# A Hero of Realms

*A Shade of Vampire, Book 20*

Bella Forrest

# Also by Bella Forrest:

## A SHADE OF VAMPIRE SERIES:

### Derek & Sofia's story:

A Shade of Vampire (Book 1)
A Shade of Blood (Book 2)
A Castle of Sand (Book 3)
A Shadow of Light (Book 4)
A Blaze of Sun (Book 5)
A Gate of Night (Book 6)
A Break of Day (Book 7)

### Rose & Caleb's story:

A Shade of Novak (Book 8)
A Bond of Blood (Book 9)
A Spell of Time (Book 10)
A Chase of Prey (Book 11)
A Shade of Doubt (Book 12)
A Turn of Tides (Book 13)
A Dawn of Strength (Book 14)
A Fall of Secrets (Book 15)
An End of Night (Book 16)

Ben & River's story:

A Wind of Change (Book 17)
A Trail of Echoes (Book 18)
A Soldier of Shadows (Book 19)
A Hero of Realms (Book 20)


## A SHADE OF KIEV TRILOGY:

A Shade of Kiev 1
A Shade of Kiev 2
A Shade of Kiev 3

## BEAUTIFUL MONSTER DUOLOGY:

Beautiful Monster 1
Beautiful Monster 2

For an updated list of Bella's books,
please visit www.bellaforrest.net

# Contents

# Chapter 1: Ben

I hadn't wanted to watch Corrine leave with River. I remained outside my bedroom until I was sure that they were gone before stepping back in.

My eyes fell on the empty mattress. The sheets where River had lain were still molded with her form. I walked to the center of the room and stopped at the edge of the bed. The deathly silence of the jinn's atrium surrounded me. A hollowness gripped my stomach.

I didn't remember ever feeling so alone in my life

as I did in that moment. Even when I had first left The Shade, my home, I'd held a glimmer of hope that I would solve my problems and be able to return.

Now it felt like I'd been flung into a void. A void where no matter how many loved ones and well-wishers waited for me, not a single one could reach me.

I breathed in. River's scent still lingered in the room.

*River.*

*She'll return to her family now and get on with her life. And hopefully, she won't be stupid enough to wait for me.*

The only semblance of a plan I had was to delay the oracle's prediction. To delay my "inevitable" end.

After all the oracle had revealed, I should've been terrified. But more than anything I just felt numb.

I realized that since I left Hortencia's cave, I'd stopped thinking of a life past the next few days, perhaps the next week. If I tried to think further ahead, I would go insane. I just had to take my life one day at a time—or better still, one hour at a time, as I tried to stave off my craving for blood.

My bedroom's emptiness eating away at me, I entered the en suite bathroom and closed the door. Gripping the sides of the sink, I raised my head and stared at my face in the mirror. *The face of a man possessed.* I moved closer to the glass. *What are you?* I stared deeper into my own eyes, as though I expected to see the shadowy creature behind them. Then again, perhaps I had already seen him. After killing, my eyes always went dark, sometimes pitch black. Perhaps that was him, his influence manifesting itself physically through me.

A chill ran down my spine. I tore my eyes away from the mirror and lowered my head to the sink, splashing my face with water.

As I straightened up, I felt a twinge in my stomach, the beginnings of a new wave of hunger. I recalled the last time I drank blood—it'd been at the jinn's lunch, when Aisha had tricked River into eating human bone. Since River had thrown up all over the floor, and I'd had to take her away, I hadn't drunk much then.

I was beginning to feel the consequences of that now.

My mind wandered to the exquisite human blood waiting for me in my kitchen. I practically salivated just thinking about it.

I left the bathroom and swept toward the kitchen. Grabbing hold of the handle of the fridge, I ripped open the door and pulled out the chilled blood.

My stomach tied itself into knots being within such close proximity of it. I wanted to drink straight from the jug, perhaps even drain the whole lot in one go. I imagined the divine liquid sliding down my throat like nectar, invigorating my senses, spreading a rush of strength through my entire body.

My hands shook with the urge to raise it to my mouth, and it was all I could do to force myself toward the kitchen sink. As much as it killed me, I tipped the jug upside down and emptied its entire contents into the basin. I turned on the tap, rinsing down the remaining traces of blood, then cleaned out the jug. I needed to ask the jinn to stop supplying me with blood.

*I'm going to have to starve myself.*

Although I'd attempted this before—with disastrous consequences—this time at least I had the jinn to assist me. I could ask them to restrain me and not let me out of my apartment no matter what I said or did.

I still didn't know exactly what would happen if a vampire starved himself—I'd always found a throat to rip through before getting close enough to find out. I wondered whether starving myself would weaken the Elder. I guessed that it would, but whether it would make him abandon our bond was another matter entirely…

I froze as there was a knock on my front door. I was surprised to be disturbed at this time of night. But whoever it was, I felt grateful for the distraction.

I hurried to the door and opened it. To my surprise, I found myself face to face with the Nasiri queen herself, Nuriya. Her expression was soft and filled with compassion as she gazed at me.

She reached out a hand, her fingers caressing the side of my face. "Oh, Benjamin," she said, her voice filled with sorrow. "Aisha told me everything. I didn't realize the situation was this bad."

I stepped away from her, in no mood to be touched. She caught my hands, and, inviting herself inside, pulled me to the living room.

"You see," she said, still holding onto me tightly even as I tried to distance myself, "we jinn know a lot of things, but even we are not all-knowing. We knew about some pieces of your past—that you had been imprinted upon by an Elder for use during their battle with Aviary all those years ago. I just didn't realize how far-reaching the consequences of that Elder's touch would be. I-I didn't know that he was—" Her voice choked up and she stifled a sob. "I didn't know that he was claiming you for himself for life." Her eyes lowered to my chest, and she eyed it as though she was trying to see through me, to the spirit within.

I was beginning to tire of her visit. All she was doing was rubbing in what I already knew.

"Would you please tell me why you're here?" I asked, in no mood to be receiving any kind of sympathy, especially not from this jinni.

I groaned internally as she wrapped her arms around me and pulled me to her in a hug. Her lips pressed against my forehead in a kiss. "Because you are my son."

As weird as I already knew she was, even I was taken aback by the intensity of emotion in her voice as she spoke.

"You're one of my own," she continued, "my dependent. We are meant to be together forever. It is my duty to see to your well-being. I-I feel like I have failed you."

I watched with a mixture of disbelief and awkwardness as a tear slipped from her eye and glided down her sculpted cheek.

Then her hold on me tightened even more. "No," she said, her voice dropping to a hiss. "He cannot take you away from me. You are mine. My child. Mine forever."

*In her own warped way, she really does consider me her son.*

I ducked my head out from under her grasp again

and created about six feet of distance between us. I wondered whether all jinn were as possessive as this queen—whether all of them developed such an attachment for their serfs, as though they'd borne them from their own womb. Or perhaps with me it was just intensified because of the bond I'd formed with her.

Whatever the case, I supposed it could only work to my advantage.

"But how will you stop us from being separated?" I asked, attempting to play on her emotions. "How will you stop him from taking me away from you? You already told me that you don't know how to help me."

Her expression turned all the more desolate. "It's true." She clung on to me yet again—as though she was addicted to physical contact. "I do not know how to solve this, Benjamin." Her chest shuddered as she drew in a rasping breath. "But I will do everything within my power to help you." Her hands began to shake, her lower lip trembling. "I will take charge of you personally."

Though her offer hardly made the situation seem less hopeless, I couldn't deny that the thought of not having to deal with Aisha any more was a small relief.

Since I was supposed to be bound to the jinn, I wondered how the Elder claiming me would work. Whether his power would just override theirs—or whether their bond would still remain, but weakened. I had no idea. I asked the question out loud to Nuriya.

"You will always be ours!" Nuriya replied, her voice now more choked up than ever.

I decided not to ask her to clarify, since she seemed close to a nervous breakdown.

"Now tell me," she said, gulping hard. "How can we help you?"

I clenched my jaw.

*I wish I knew.*

# Chapter 2: River

I woke up to a cool breeze blowing over me. When I opened my eyes, to my confusion, I felt sand beneath me. I wondered whether I was dreaming. The last thing I remembered, I'd been in Ben's bed, lying in his arms and relishing the feel of his palm stroking my forehead.

Now I was on a beach. A long, dark beach.

Corrine was kneeling over me, a look of concern on her face.

"Where are we?" I asked. "Where's Ben?"

Corrine didn't answer as I stood up. Too fast. The blood rushed from my head. I felt dizzy and had to sit back down again. I realized now that I was still in my underwear.

"Put this on," Corrine said, her voice soft and kind. She held my dress, the light cotton one that I'd changed into back in Ben's apartment. She pulled the dress over my head and guided my arms through the sleeves.

As the veil of sleep lifted from me, Corrine didn't need to answer my questions. A heaviness weighed down my chest. My voice became constricted. "Ben... He's still in The Oasis," I breathed. "He told you to bring me back, didn't he?"

Corrine bit her lip, and tears moistened the corners of her eyes. She nodded, and tucked a stray strand of hair behind my ear.

"I'm sorry, sweetie," she said. "I tried to make him reconsider... but this was what he wanted."

My breath hitched.

I played over in my mind the moments we had shared before I'd fallen into slumber. I could hardly say that this came as a complete surprise. His mood … It had reminded me too much of the night he'd let go of my hand. I'd sensed that he was going to make me leave him—sooner or later—even as he'd held me in his arms and kissed my lips like he would never let me go. But although I'd expected it to happen, I hadn't thought that it would be so sudden, while I wasn't even awake to say goodbye.

"What is he going to do?" I managed.

Corrine shook her head. "He wasn't sure."

How could he be sure? From what the oracle told us, I had no idea where he would even start—if there even was any place to start—or whether he would just come to accept what she had claimed was his destiny.

I felt sick to my stomach as Corrine wrapped an arm around my waist and helped me to my feet. Still not steady enough to stand, I clung to her as we left the beach and entered a familiar clearing behind the jetty.

Emotions overwhelmed me. I already felt like I was in mourning for Ben. And I hated myself for it—that I could give up all hope so easily. I just didn't know where to draw hope from when every door around us seemed to be shut.

I could barely pay attention to Corrine's words. She muttered something about taking me to my family. She vanished us again, and we reappeared in the center of some kind of town square.

"This is The Vale," Corrine said in a hushed tone. "The humans' residences."

She led me across the square and toward a townhouse near a fountain. A warm light was emanating from one of the windows. She knocked softly on the door and waited.

A woman wearing pajamas answered the door. A human, I could tell by the scent of her. She had long, straight black hair and was apparently in her mid-thirties. Her eyes shifted from me to the witch.

"Corrine?" the woman said, sounding surprised.

"Anna," the witch replied. "I'm so sorry to disturb you at this time of night."

"Where have you been?" Anna interrupted, moving forward and clasping Corrine's shoulder. "Ibrahim has been going insane with worry. He's searched for you everywhere. We all have."

"I was trapped in The Oasis," Corrine replied. "I got caught and, well... it's a long story. I'm sure there will be time for me to give you the full explanation, but for now, I wondered if you know where River's family is being housed on the island?"

"Oh, yes." A smile broke out on Anna's face, her eyes falling to me again. "We actually offered to take them into our own home. We cleared out two of the bedrooms upstairs. Your mother and siblings are up there sleeping right now."

Corrine let out a sigh of relief. "Perfect," she said. The witch looked back down at me with kind, sorrowful eyes. "Are you okay to go with Anna now?"

I nodded, my throat too tight to answer.

Anna reached for my hand and took it, leading me inside the house.

"Good night, Corrine," she said.

"Good night," the witch replied, before vanishing from the spot.

Anna closed the door.

"How are you feeling?" she asked. "Would you like

something to drink? Are you hungry?"

I was relieved that she didn't start asking me about my time in The Oasis. I could have done with some water, but I was in no mood for anything at all. I shook my head.

"Thanks," I croaked.

"Okay," she said. She led me up the staircase to a spacious landing. She pointed to two doors—one directly in front of me, and one at the end of the corridor on the right-hand side.

"Your mom and sisters are in this one, and your brother is in the room on the right. His room is pretty small, but there's room for another mattress in your mom's room. I suggest you go in there."

"Okay."

She moved to the door in front of us, and knocked. I could hear the sounds of my family sleeping. I should've felt happy at the thought of seeing their faces again. But I just felt numb.

Anna knocked more loudly when nobody answered. "Nadia?" she called.

There was the creak of a mattress, and then the

door opened. My mother stood before us in a lilac nightie, her hair tied in a braid that hung down one shoulder. "River!" she gasped before smothering me in a hug.

Anna went about arranging for another mattress and more bedding to be brought into the room. It was her husband, Kyle—a kind-looking man with grey-peppered hair—who helped her carry it all inside. My mother thanked them profusely before they bid us goodnight and left us alone.

My sisters had woken up during the shuffle, and as I sank down on my mattress, the three of them gathered around me. They asked me dozens of questions—what had happened? Why was I back? Would I stay? I answered them as patiently as I could while giving the least amount of detail.

"Let's get some rest now," my mother said, apparently sensing my mind was someplace else. "We'll have plenty of time to talk in the morning."

She kissed my forehead before ushering my sisters back into bed. Then she switched off the lights, plunging the room into darkness.

Despite the moderate temperature of the room, a wave of coldness swept through my bones. Gripping my blanket, I enveloped myself in it. I curled up in a fetal position. The same position I had been in just hours ago, when Ben had been holding me.

Through the pain, I thought about what he'd said the first time he'd tried to leave me. He'd said if I returned to The Shade, I could get on with my life, and perhaps live here in safety with my family.

When the idea of moving to The Shade had first occurred to me, I'd barely been able to contain my excitement.

Now, as much as I reminded myself of the wonder and beauty of the place, without Ben, it felt like any other.

# Chapter 3: Corrine

After taking River to her family in the Vale, I had to find my husband. I vanished myself from Anna's house and reappeared in the Sanctuary, directly outside Ibrahim's and my bedroom. I placed my ear against the door, straining to hear my husband's breathing. I couldn't. Turning the handle, I pushed the door open and switched on the light. The room was empty. But it was more than empty. It was… an absolute wreck.

My eyes widened. Ibrahim had a habit of not

tidying up after himself and leaving things scattered about—but this… this was a level of messiness that I hadn't thought even my husband was capable of. The room had been turned upside down. All the contents of the drawers had been emptied—piles of books, clothes and papers all over the floor—the curtains were awry, and the mattress and bedsheets had been ripped from the bed. Heck, even the rug was scrunched up in one corner.

My pulse raced. *What happened here?*

I shot out of the door and began hurrying along the hallways from room to room. Each of them were in a similar state of disarray. Not even the bathrooms had been spared.

As I entered the chaotic living room, meeting with a similar state of mess, I was relieved to see my husband sitting in an armchair, his back to me. His head rested in his hand, and from the way he breathed, it was clear he'd fallen asleep upright.

His face was rough and unshaven, and even as he slept, he looked utterly exhausted. *My poor baby.* I guessed that the state of our home was a result of his attempt to try to figure out where I'd gone, thinking perhaps I'd left behind a clue. I knelt down before him and placed my hand over his right forearm, which rested on his lap. I squeezed it gently. He twitched, and then his head lifted from his hand. His eyelids flickered open. I almost laughed at the way his eyes bulged as he looked at me. I was sure that he thought he was still dreaming.

"Corrine!"

"Darling," I said, beaming at him. He stood up and engulfed me in his arms. Clutching the back of my head, he pushed his lips against mine and kissed me passionately.

"How are you here?" he gasped.

Letting out a sigh, I pulled him down on the sofa with me and began telling him everything that had happened since I'd left The Shade. Recounting Ben's story was the hardest part. What the oracle had told them, what she'd predicted would happen to him… I had to pause several times to keep my voice from cracking.

By the time I'd finished, Ibrahim's mouth was

hanging open.

"Now I've seen you," I said, "I must urgently speak to Sofia and Derek. They need to know what happened to their son, and what he's up against."

To my surprise, Ibrahim shook his head. "They're not here. They left along with Rose, Caleb, Aiden and dozens of other vampires, as well as all our dragons."

"What? When?"

"According to Jeriad, the dragons used to have some understanding with the jinn. He said that he knows where their realm is in the supernatural world, and they had ties with one of the families that lived there. They've gone to see if they can find a way to get Ben out of this bond between him and The Oasis' jinn."

"Oh." My heart sank. I wished that I had managed to return before they left. "D-Do you know when they will be returning?"

Ibrahim shrugged. "How could I—or they— possibly predict that?"

"One couldn't," I muttered.

The thought of having to wait an undetermined amount of time to tell Ben's parents the news about him being bound to an Elder was hard to swallow. But there was no way I could go after them to tell them. I had no idea where they would be by now, so I had no choice but to wait.

As harrowing as the thought was, and as much as I tried to ignore it, I couldn't help but think that their whole mission to try to break Ben's bond with the jinn might be a waste anyway. At least, if the oracle's prediction came true, the jinn were the very least of Benjamin's worries.

I paused, trying to turn my mind to other thoughts.

"So they left with every single one of our dragons?" I said.

"That was what Jeriad wanted. And all the witches stayed behind."

"Of course," I murmured.

I certainly didn't feel comfortable about them facing those devious, magical creatures without a single witch by their side, but I supposed that at least they had the horde of dragons—whatever good they were against the jinn.

My mind wandered back to Ben. I looked at Ibrahim. "I think Derek and Sofia should be the first on this island to know about what happened to Ben. It just wouldn't feel right to tell anyone else before they returned. So for now, let's just keep this between you and me. I'll tell River the same thing... though I can't imagine her wanting to talk about this topic with anyone."

"I agree," Ibrahim replied. "It's only right that they should know first."

I leaned back in the sofa and looked around the distressed living room. Now, I didn't know what else we could do but wait for their return. Although I certainly had no intention of sitting here idle. Once I'd whipped our home back into a state of sanity, I was going to sit in my library and scour every single one of my hundreds of books that could possibly contain information about the Elders.

Although if I was being honest with myself, I knew that such an exercise would be just that—an exercise, to pass the time. To make me feel like I was doing something. To make me feel like I wasn't helpless.

Because deep down, I knew. Not a single one of the hundreds of books I possessed would contain the solution for Benjamin.

# Chapter 4: Ben

I stared at the jinni hovering in front of me. As the hunger continued to rise in my stomach, at least for now, there was only one thing that I could think to ask for.

"I need you to contain me in this apartment," I said. "Lock the doors from the outside and reinforce them so that I can't get out, no matter how hard I slam against the doors or walls."

Nuriya looked perturbed. "But that can't be the answer, Benjamin," she said. "You can't just solve the problem by locking yourself up."

"I know," I said, grimacing. "I know. But I need some time to gather my thoughts. I can't afford to risk spiraling out of control again and breaking into the human prison upstairs."

"All right," she said, still looking uncertain. "It will be done. Nobody will disturb you, and you will not be able to get out."

With that, after clutching me to her once again, she disappeared from the room.

Of course, even the jinn locking me in here wasn't a foolproof plan—especially now I no longer had River to help keep my thirst in check. When in the deepest throes of my bloodlust, I lost control over my actions. I had navigated a submarine from adrift in the ocean all the way up to a beach, where I'd murdered several people. I'd only realized what I'd done once I'd returned. Once it took hold of me again, all I had to do was brush against my snake bracelet and ask the jinni to let me out. I didn't see a way to prevent this—I wasn't about to ask them to stop fulfilling my requests. I just had to hope that I could come up with my next step before I descended that far.

I moved back into my bedroom and resumed my seat on the edge of the bed. I closed my eyes and rubbed my temples.

If even the all-seeing oracle couldn't offer me any advice as to what to do, I couldn't imagine who else would be able to. If there was any way out of this, it was clear that I had only myself to rely on.

I played over my visit to the oracle's cave in my mind, recalling every detail in case I had missed some crucial piece of information amid the shock I'd been in at the time.

My brain focused on what the oracle had said the repercussions could be if—or when—the Elder's plan came about. She'd said that if he managed to use me to nurse his soul back to full health, it would be easy for him to bring the rest of his kind back to strength. *Especially with my help.* I preferred not to think about how exactly they'd use me, though I could guess.

But if he was successful in bringing the rest of his kind back to strength, what would this mean? From what I understood, the Hawks had been their only true adversaries, or at least the only ones to be reckoned with. But after the war that had taken place between the two species, the Hawks' influence had been diminished to nothing. I didn't know what would stop the Elders from rising to prominence once again. By now, I was sure that they must've become aware that not all the gates had been closed eighteen years ago, and some still remained today. If they managed to regain their former vitality, there would be nothing stopping them from reentering the human realm and wreaking havoc once again. Only this time I imagined it would be far, far worse because no Hawks would be there to hinder them.

My parents had spoken of the horrors of the time when the Elders had taken over The Shade. The devastation they'd caused. The lives they had ripped apart.

*No. That can't happen again. It just can't.*

And yet here I'd been, with each gulp of blood I took, bringing this threat closer to reality.

As I sat there alone in that silent bedroom, it

became clear to me that far more than just my life hung in the balance. And the more I thought about it, it wasn't even the lives of everyone I loved in The Shade either. No. This was a much, much greater fight.

The entire human realm could be threatened by these spirits' need for human blood. And from what I knew, the Elders posed great danger even to other supernatural realms.

My head reeled at the implications if I allowed myself to consume even a few more liters of blood. The consequences that could follow for all realms.

All of this rested on my shoulders. My shaky, unsteady shoulders.

Through the confusion I'd been in, one thing became crystal clear as I sat there in the early hours of the morning:

I had to thwart the Elders' plan... no matter what the sacrifice.

# Chapter 5: Derek

It was no surprise that all of our closest companions immediately volunteered to come with us on our journey with the dragons. As we stood in the clearing preparing to take off, I was surrounded by my family and friends. Sofia and Aiden stood by my side. A few feet away was Rose with Caleb, the Novalics, Ashley and Landis, Zinnia and Gavin, and dozens of other familiar faces. Even Cameron—always the fearless warrior—had offered to come with us, even though he was still a human. Of course, we'd declined his offer.

Apart from witches, Jeriad had also thought that it was better that no werewolves came with us. I wasn't sure why that was—why jinn had a particular dislike for wolves compared to vampires—but I didn't bother pressing for an answer.

It had dawned on me that I possessed a magic of sort—the ability to conjure fire from my palms. A power that I had inherited from the great witch Cora. But Jeriad didn't mention there being a problem with me coming, so I didn't mention it either.

As soon as everyone was gathered, Ibrahim along with three other witches cast a spell of shadow over all the vampires. Since we were traveling atop the dragons' backs, we would be exposed to the sun. We just had to hope that this spell would last until we returned.

Then we each climbed on top of the dragons— most of us traveling in pairs. Sofia and I rode Jeriad, who was the first to launch into the sky, leading the horde upward, high into the clouds. It was important to me that we gained altitude before crossing the boundary, because I didn't want the hunters spotting us.

Once we had flown high enough and exited the boundary, the dragons picked up speed.

Jeriad had been cryptic about what we would find on reaching the realm of the jinn, and he still hadn't given any description about the place itself—except that supernaturals called it The Dunes.

It didn't take long for the dragons to begin descending again, for we were going to be passing through a gate that was close to The Shade. It was situated in an old, dried-up well on a small island that Caleb and Rose had once been stranded on with Annora. Rose had the misfortune of passing through this very gate, having been kidnapped and carried down there by the prince of ogres. Indeed, it led to the realm of the ogres. I wasn't entirely happy about using this gate, but it was the gate the dragons had initially passed through on coming to the human realm, and they were comfortable with it. So we found ourselves descending to the jungle-infested island.

The dragons ended up crushing many of the trees in the surrounding area as they landed. We climbed off their backs before they shifted back into their humanoid forms—for there was no way they could have fit through the gate while in their dragon forms. I caught Sofia's hand, and we all gathered around the small well. I couldn't help but look at my daughter's face. Her expression was a mixture of nostalgia and horror. I could only imagine how traumatic that experience must've been for her.

I pushed to the front with Jeriad, Sofia following behind me.

"Three of us dragons should pass through first." Jeriad spoke up. "Just in case there are any ogres on the other side."

Jeriad and the others passed through the gate first. After that, Sofia and I followed, and as we landed on the other side, we found ourselves on a beach lined with high, sinister-looking walls, connected by a massive iron gate spiked with what appeared to be skulls. Human skulls. The wind was harsh and chilled even me.

As the dragons passed through the gate and landed on the beach beside us, they began shifting back into their beastly forms. Jeriad had already shifted back, having arrived before us. I was about to suggest to Sofia that we climb onto his back again, but as we approached, he spread his wings and took off into the sky before we could climb up.

"Jeriad?" Sofia called after him, her brows furrowed in confusion. We both stared as he shot toward a patch of trees in the distance. We sped up to follow him, trying to see what he was aiming for, and soon enough it became clear. There was a choked roar—a roar that wasn't loud enough for a dragon's—and Jeriad lifted himself back into the sky, clasping a giant ogre between his jaws. The ogre flailed wildly, only causing the dragon to clamp down harder.

More dragons took Jeriad's cue, except— apparently not finding any more ogres on the beach—they began to fly over the walls.

"What are they doing?" Ashley asked.

The dragons didn't take long to return. Each carried

an ogre as they soared back over the walls. They touched down on the sand before tearing into the ogres' flesh with their mighty jaws. I'd seen many gruesome things in my life, but this made even me queasy.

"It's a good thing that Brett and Bella aren't here to witness this," Sofia muttered. "I doubt they'd ever sleep at night again."

As Jeriad tore through his ogre's gut, spilling a load of foul-smelling intestines, I caught Sofia's waist and turned our backs on the scene. The other vampires followed my lead. We approached the waves and stared out toward the ocean. A much more pleasant view. It was clear to me now why the dragons had been so bent on arriving through this particular gate…

I turned toward Ashley—who looked close to throwing up—and belatedly answered her question. "Just a little lunch break."

*** 

Once the dragons had finished their meal, they flew into the ocean and washed off the blood. Then, rising from the waves, the horde landed back on the beach.

I looked toward Jeriad. "Finished?"

"Apologies," he growled. "It's been a while since we tasted ogre… And who knows when we might taste it again."

We passed by the huge corpses scattered about the beach—stripped to the bone—and remounted the dragons. Sofia positioned herself behind me, wrapping her arms around my waist. I felt her shudder against me as we launched back into the sky.

"That was so gross," she muttered.

I chuckled. I was happy to see her mood a little lighter since she'd found out about Jeriad's proposal. Although there was no guarantee that we would be able to help our son get free from the jinn, we had confidence in the dragons. And at the very least, this escapade gave us the feeling that we were doing something rather than just sitting idle back on the island.

I looked downward. The dragons were moving swiftly away from the land of the ogres, so I didn't get much of a chance to take in the landscape. We found ourselves soaring over a sprawling mass of water. Although it was daytime, it was surprisingly dark— the sky was overcast, and I didn't remember ever seeing such thick clouds. As the dragons gained altitude, the water beneath us disappeared, and we were engulfed by the thick fog.

Sofia's arms tightened around me a little, and her cool lips brushed against the back of my neck. "I love you, Derek," she whispered.

A small smile formed on my lips. Detaching her arms from me, I wrapped an arm around her and shifted her so that she sat in front of me, her back against my chest. I wanted to hold her rather than have her hold me. Engulfing her small waist in my arms, I kissed the side of her face before whispering into her ear:

"I don't blame you."

She smirked, nudging me gently in the stomach with the back of her elbow. Then she swiveled on the dragon's back until both of her legs hung over one side. Now that she could face me better, she wrapped her arms around my neck and pulled me down for a long, deep kiss. I reached a hand into her warm auburn hair and closed my eyes, relishing the taste of her lips. *My girl.* Despite being married for almost two decades now, that was still how I thought of her. The bold, beautiful, self-willed girl I'd woken up to after four hundred years of sleep.

I ran a hand from her waist down the curve of her hip and along her thigh, my kisses growing more demanding. The thick clouds surrounding us made me feel as though we were in our own little bubble. Though I could sense the others flying nearby, we couldn't see them, and Jeriad's head was set forward, many feet away from us. It almost felt as though we were alone, drifting through these clouds. Just the two of us.

We spent the next few hours of the journey wrapped in each other's arms, enjoying every moment of this opportunity to be with each other completely uninterrupted by the rest of the world.

# Chapter 6: Ben

The oracle had told me in no uncertain terms that it wasn't possible to exorcise this Elder in the way that others had been exorcised. For one thing, his influence had been ingrained in my system for too long. That meant there was only one option:

Somehow, he had to decide to abandon me.

I had to make things so difficult and uncomfortable for this spirit that he chose to do so of his own accord.

I racked my brain as to what I could possibly do to

bring this about. Each time, the idea I came back to was… Starvation. It was the only logical thing I could think of. The reason he had bonded with me to begin with was to use me for blood. If I didn't give him what he wanted, what reason would he have to stay within me? I had no idea whether it would work, but at this point, I'd crossed the brink of desperation. There was nothing else on the table, and no hope of any other idea coming soon, so I had no choice but to attempt it.

Brushing the golden snake band around my wrist, I summoned Nuriya to me once again. There was a look of relief and trepidation on her face.

"What have you decided?" she asked.

"I need you to take me far away from any humans, preferably still somewhere underground, and lock me up. You will leave me, and if I summon you and ask you to give me human blood, you're not to give it to me."

She hesitated. "For how long will you stay away?"

I gritted my teeth. *As long as it takes.* "I don't know," I replied.

"Have you thought about the effect starving yourself might have on you?"

I nodded, even though I hadn't been able to think about it. I wasn't sure what effect starvation had on vampires… But now it seemed I had no choice but to find out.

"Well, I'm not comfortable about my child going hungry," Nuriya said, "but if you really want to try this… I know somewhere I can take you. It's in the desert, many miles away from here. A little hideout I created underground for myself—I still go there every now and then when I want time alone."

"Perfect," I said.

"Do you want to leave now?"

"Yes. Now."

A few moments later, I found myself standing with Nuriya in a spacious room tiled with black marble. There was a deep red rug in the center, a bed in one corner, and a sitting area with shelves filled with books of some kind. There was also a desk and chair, and even a small dining table for two.

"The bathroom is through there," she said,

pointing to a door behind me.

I breathed in, pleased by what I sensed. It seemed that we were very far away from any humans—I couldn't detect even the slightest trace of human blood, unlike in the jinn's atrium where the prison was situated just above it.

"This will do fine," I said.

"There are some books over there, some of them in English," she said. "But I'm not sure what else you'll do to entertain yourself all day."

As the hunger pangs in my stomach intensified, the very last thing on my mind was entertaining myself. I just needed to survive.

Nuriya kissed the top of my head. "Goodbye, Benjamin."

"Remember," I said, looking at her sternly, "no blood—no matter how much I beg."

She appeared reluctant, and something told me that she might even disobey my request and come to spy on me to check that I was still holding up. That I didn't mind so much, as long as she didn't do anything to jeopardize my fast.

Humans could survive for weeks without food; I was about to find out how long a vampire could live without blood. But one thing I did know was that I had to push myself to the very edge—perhaps even past it—if I stood any chance of getting rid of this Elder. That was why I couldn't afford to be interrupted. I had to try to weaken him again after all the blood I'd fed him since I'd turned into a vampire. I had to try to make him feel a sense of hopelessness—that I might never drink blood again, and would prefer to starve myself to death rather than keep nourishing him.

Nuriya disappeared, and I found myself standing alone in the center of that large room. It felt like I was in possession of a deadly virus. I just had to contain myself. Keep myself away from everyone. And try to stamp it out before I could infect the rest of the world with it.

I walked over to the bookshelf and pulled down an armful of the English titles that I saw stacked there before taking a seat in an armchair. They were novels mostly—old classics. I wasn't sure where Nuriya had gotten these from—I was surprised that she even read human literature. But whatever the case, I was glad to have books for company.

I looked over the books, wondering which to start with. My eyes fell on *Heart of Darkness,* by Joseph Conrad. *A fitting title.* I ended up choosing something else and spent the next few hours reading—or at least, what felt like the next few hours. There was no clock in this place, which I was thankful for. Keeping track of time would only make the experience more agonizing.

If this ended up being successful, and the Elder did decide to leave me, I didn't know how I would be certain of it without a glass of animal blood to try... I'd never experienced what it was like to be a normal, non-possessed vampire. But I suspected that I would feel the difference in my bones.

But I couldn't allow myself to get my hopes up too much. So I tried to shut down my mind and immerse myself in the book in my lap.

As time drew on, however, my concentration dimmed, the hunger in my stomach beginning to roar too loudly for me to keep ignoring. It had been less than two days since I'd last tasted blood. I hadn't even been fasting long. I'd never had reason to starve myself before, but I was sure that humans didn't feel this much discomfort when fasting from food. It seemed that vampires abstaining from blood was far more painful.

I set my book down on the table beside me and leaned back in the chair. I was about to close my eyes and see if sleep might take me when my vision became oddly shrouded. Looking down at the book, I could barely read the letters in the title. And then, as if I had just closed my eyes, a blackness flooded my brain.

# Chapter 7: Ben

*Low-hanging branches whipped against my face as I raced through a dark wood. Hunger clawed at my stomach. My mouth was parched. Every muscle in my body felt tired and strained. I didn't know how much longer I could keep running without sustenance. And yet I couldn't slow my feet down. It was as though they belonged to someone else and, if anything, my speed only seemed to be increasing.*

I need to drink, or I'm going to pass out.

*I held my breath as the gushing of a river met my*

*ears. It was close. Very close. A scent pervaded the atmosphere as I neared. A sweet, unearthly scent. My mouth salivated as I raced harder. A clearing came into view, beyond which ran a river. A crimson river. I could barely contain myself as I knelt down on the edge of the bank. I cupped my hands and dipped them into the red liquid. I swallowed a mouthful. It tasted even more divine than it smelt. It glided down my throat like nectar. As I downed gulp after gulp, it felt like it was invigorating every cell in my body. By the time I stood up again, my hunger fully satiated, I felt like a new person. Strong. Invincible. Like I could do anything with these refreshed limbs. Take on a thousand armed hunters, run the circumference of the globe...*

A stabbing sensation in my arms brought me to consciousness. There was a disgusting taste in my mouth, nothing like the succulent taste in my dream. My vision came back to me. Frowning, I looked down.

My heart skipped a beat.

My arms were pierced with deep, oozing puncture marks. The blood had dripped onto my lap and stained the seat. I reached a hand to my mouth. It felt moist. When I withdrew my fingers, they too were covered with the red substance.

I went to the bathroom and stared at myself in the mirror, my face, body and clothes a bloody mess.

*I've just been cannibalizing myself.*

I bent over the sink and rinsed my mouth out, horrified at the taste of my own blood. Then I stripped off my soiled clothes and turned on the shower. Stepping inside, I washed away the stains from my face, chest, and arms. Now that the blood was rinsed off, I could see exactly what damage I'd done to myself. The scattering of puncture wounds were in the process of healing, though they were taking longer than they should.

I stepped out of the shower and dried myself off. Wrapping a robe around my body, I looked at myself again in the mirror. Now that I was no longer distracted by the blood coating my mouth, I noticed the difference in my eyes. They had become darker. Much darker. There was hardly a tint of green left in them.

Tearing my gaze away, I walked back into the main

room. My body felt weaker than ever. The dream that I'd had—imagining myself consuming endless amounts of exquisite blood—only made the reality more unbearable.

My knees unsteady, I stared at the red-stained fabric of the armchair I'd been sitting in.

*How can I stop myself from doing that again?*

I cast my gaze around the room, looking for anything that I might be able to use to restrain myself. But I couldn't see anything suitable.

I had no choice but to summon the jinni again.

Nuriya looked strained as she appeared after five minutes, her eyes fixing on the blood.

"I fell into some kind of… daze just now," I began, before she could utter a word. I was sure that it hadn't been sleep, because my eyes hadn't been closed—just fogged over. "I started drinking my own blood. I need you to make sure that doesn't happen again. Restrain me somehow…"

"Restrain you," she murmured.

"Maybe even fix me to the wall if you have to," I said.

"No, no," she said, shaking her head. "That won't be necessary. And besides, it would be far too uncomfortable."

She moved closer to me and cupped my face in her hands. At first I thought this was just her usual irritating, overly-affectionate behavior, and I was about to brush her aside, but from her expression of concentration I realized that she was doing something else. When she let go of me, I raised a hand to my face but found that, no matter how hard I tried, I couldn't bring it closer than five inches from my mouth. I tried to raise my forearm and bring it closer, but again, it was impossible. It was as though she had placed an invisible barrier around my head.

*This should do the job.*

I looked toward her and nodded, grateful for the solution. "Thank you," I said. "You can leave again now."

She glanced at the blood and as she did, the stains vanished from the seat, as if they had never been there to begin with. Then, after saying goodbye, she left.

Alone again, I heaved a sigh. Now it was time to wait again. I didn't attempt to pick up another book—my hunger was far too blinding for me to be able to concentrate. Instead I walked over to the bed and lay down. Maybe, if I could just drift back into unconsciousness, I would be able to pass more time like this. Now that I was no longer able to harm myself with my fangs, this would be the least painful state of existence.

# Chapter 8: Ben

By some mercy, I did manage to sleep. I didn't remember the last time I'd rested properly, and my body was exhausted.

When I woke up, it was with a strange lightness in my head. As I sat up and looked around the room, my vision was sharp and crisp. I stood up, and when I felt a sense of strength in my body, I wondered whether I was just imagining it. I stretched out my arms, examining them. They had healed by now. I wondered how long I'd been asleep.

I walked around the room, allowing the last traces of sleep to leave me. As they did, I became suddenly aware of the absence of the acute hunger that had been plaguing me before. I still felt thirst—but it wasn't even half as uncomfortable.

I entered the bathroom and splashed my face with cold water. When I glanced up at the mirror, my eyes had returned to their normal vivid green color.

*Perhaps more time has passed than it feels like?*

I held my breath, unsure of what to think. I wondered whether this was just my wishful thinking carrying me away—making me read signs. I didn't want to get my hopes up even in the slightest that something might've changed.

I left the bathroom and walked back into the main room. I continued pacing up and down, paying close attention to the level of hunger in my stomach and my general state of being. Perhaps this was just the effect of having rested for a long time—my body was rejuvenated, but soon the effect would wear off and the pangs would grow strong and loud again.

I kept pacing the room, waiting for the agony to

strike again. But it didn't. All I felt was the type of hunger that a human might experience—uncomfortable, but not unbearable. Not anywhere near the level I had gotten used to experiencing as a vampire—the type that could make me lose my mind. *Or make me start biting into my own flesh…*

I still didn't dare voice my hope inside my head, because reading the signs wrong would only make the disappointment all the more crushing.

But after several hours of monitoring my level of hunger, and paying close attention to the way I was feeling in general, there was a test that I wanted to carry out.

I brushed a hand against the snake's head on my wrist band and waited for Nuriya to appear. She arrived after a few minutes.

Her eyes widened as she looked me over. "You're looking better," she said.

I winced internally at her words, still so tentative about letting myself entertain the idea. I just wanted to focus on the test—which would give us a hard result either way without speculation or false hope.

"I want you to feed me some animal blood," I said.

Nuriya moved toward the dining area in one corner of the spacious room and turned her back on me. She pulled down a glass and a jug from one of the shelves. When she turned around, the jug that she was holding was filled with red liquid.

She handed me the glass, and then filled it to the top.

"What kind of blood is this?" I asked, raising the glass to my nose so I could sniff it.

"Snake blood," she replied.

I remembered the last time I'd tried to drink snake blood. I'd gone into the snake room in the upper atrium. I had ended up throwing up all over the floor.

Gingerly, I raised the glass to my lips and took my first sip.

I felt like gagging the moment the liquid entered my mouth. It was so repugnant, so eye-wateringly bitter to my palate after the rich, luxuriant human blood The Oasis had afforded me. I wouldn't have been surprised if I vomited from the taste alone.

But I managed to hold it down. I downed another gulp, larger this time, holding my nose as I swallowed. And then I took a third gulp. A fourth. A fifth. Until I had finished one and a half glasses of the blood.

I hurried to the bathroom and rinsed my mouth out in an attempt to get rid of the disgusting aftertaste before returning to the main room and sitting down on the edge of the bed.

The jinni was watching me closely. "How are you feeling?" she asked.

I held up a hand, breathing deeply. It was too early for me to say. When I'd last tried to drink blood, it had taken a while for my body to expel it—at least a few minutes. During those minutes I had allowed myself to hope, falsely. I wasn't about to do that again.

"Ask me again in fifteen minutes," I said, eyeing her diamond-encrusted wrist watch.

She took a seat on the sofa, opposite from me, and the two of us sat in intense silence. I leaned forward, resting my elbows against my knees, and closed my eyes, trying to feel what this animal blood was doing to me. I hadn't vomited by the time Nuriya told me that fifteen minutes had gone by.

I tried to remember how many minutes it had taken for me to throw up before. If I remembered right, it was certainly less than five.

I moved over to the dining table and tipped the blood remaining in the jug into the glass. Slowly, I knocked down the rest of it. Every last drop. And then I waited again for another fifteen minutes.

Despite the taste, I was still showing no signs of expelling the blood.

"I'd like to drink some more," I said. I wanted to fill myself up with as much blood as I possibly could, so that there could be absolutely no doubt in my mind as to the conclusion of the test.

"Why don't we return to our kitchen then?" she asked. "You can sit there and drink as much blood as you need, my child."

I agreed. She made smoke surround us and the next thing I knew, I was standing in the middle of the jinn's huge kitchen. It was empty now, the fragrance of a recently cooked meal flavoring the air.

She pointed to a table and chair in one of the corners, upon which stood a large round, steel container of blood, a label hanging from its edge. Nuriya reached up to one of the shelves and took down a tall glass. As I took a seat at the table, she set it down in front of me. She squeezed my shoulder. "Drink to your heart's content, Benjamin."

"But stay with me," I said. I wasn't ready for her to leave just yet.

I began making my way through the vat of liquid—but I only managed three more full glasses. I'd consumed a lot more human blood than that in one go before. I hoped that this was just something normal for vampires in general—they couldn't hold in as much animal blood as they could human blood—and not specifically a problem with me.

After downing as much as I could, I stood up slowly, trying not to unsettle my stomach.

"I'm going to return to my apartment now," I said.

A smile spread across the jinni's face. "Splendid," she said, a trace of relief in her voice.

We parted ways. I returned to my quarters and locked myself inside. I walked the length of the corridor and entered the living room. I wasn't sure how many liters of blood I'd just downed, but I couldn't deny that my stomach was full. I didn't feel even the least twinge of hunger—I felt… satiated.

For the first time, I let go of my resistance to hope and couldn't help but begin to believe something might've changed. It'd been about an hour since snake blood had first touched my lips, and my body wasn't displaying even the slightest sign of expelling it.

***

I spent the rest of the day locked up in my apartment. I found myself instinctively avoiding the bedroom— the last place I'd spent time here with River—and stayed mostly in the living room. The fear that I was going to upchuck any second began to subside, and a feeling of confidence built within me.

Once evening arrived, I stepped outside my apartment. I moved toward the direction of the kitchen, and as it came within view, I was glad to see that the door was open. From where I was standing, it was dark, and there was apparently nobody inside. It was late enough for them to have already finished cooking dinner and, from the sounds coming from the dining hall further along, the Nasiri family were all feasting merrily.

I made my way along the veranda and slipped into the kitchen. The blood I'd consumed earlier had settled down now, making room for some more. I was bent on consuming as much as possible, today and over the next few days, until every shadow of doubt that remained in my mind was cleared.

I looked around the kitchen for the container of blood. Previously, it had sat on one of the counters, but it had been moved. I cast my eyes about and spotted the entrance to a pantry. I moved toward the door and pushed it open. I was at the top of a small flight of stairs leading down to a cold storage area. Descending into it, I passed by huge sacks of white powder—which I soon realized was ground human bone—along with an assortment of whole human bones, stripped of all flesh and hanging from the ceiling by ropes. I was worried that the sight would disturb my stomach, so I averted my eyes and continued looking around for the snake blood. I found the container eventually—it had been stored right at the back of the pantry. I picked it up and carried it back up into the kitchen. I sat down, poured myself a glass, and began to drink.

As I listened in to the cheerful conversation going on next door, a sense of excitement rose within me. Even though I was still bound to the jinn, the thought of finally being rid of the Elder left me feeling high. Although I couldn't live back in The Shade, I could at least request to visit River, my family and friends. And while I was there, if this problem was truly solved, I could mix freely with everyone and roam the island that was my home for the first time in many months.

I drank the blood much quicker this time, downing it confidently, until once again I felt satiated and could drink no more. Although the blood tasted revolting, the sheer relief that I was able to ingest it made me almost forget about the taste.

I'd never thought in my life that I would relish such a vile substance the way I did that snake blood. Every gulp felt miraculous.

Once I finished drinking, I picked up the container again and carried it back toward the pantry. Passing a sink along the way, I dropped my dirty glass into it. I placed the blood right at the back of the storage room where I'd found it and re-entered the kitchen.

Now I planned to return to my apartment, rest for a few hours, and then come back down yet again after the break to drink some more—as much as my stomach could hold.

But as I moved toward the exit of the kitchen, I realized just what a fool I'd been.

The very moment I passed by the narrow staircase that led to the atrium above, it started as a slight irritation at the back of my throat. Then it developed into a cough, until before I knew it, I was doubled over and retching. It happened so fast, so violently, and I was expelling so much, the floor was soon a pool of undigested blood.

My vision blurred and became shrouded.

A familiar heaviness settled in my chest.

I barely registered what happened next. All I could feel was the rage of hunger ripping through my stomach, making my entire body shake. A hunger so powerful, there was no room for any thought in my mind other than how to satisfy it.

My legs jolted forward up the staircase leading to the human prison. Reaching the top, I barged through the gap between the wall and the cupboard that concealed the entrance to the jinn's abode. I staggered out into the storage room, tore open the door, and appeared in a dark narrow corridor. I lunged for the nearest cell, smashing through the door with uncontrollable strength, and all that followed was a blur of red, punctuated by screaming and pervaded by smooth, rich liquid coursing down my throat. The nectar I could never live without.

# CHAPTER 9: BEN

The euphoria that pulsed through my body was indescribable. My senses felt heightened, every nerve electrified, satisfaction filling every fiber of my being. It was as though my very bones groaned with relief.

After my fangs withdrew from a particularly tender body, I stood up, my chest heaving. I didn't know how many throats I had ripped open. All I knew was that I'd drunk as much as I wanted.

My legs jolted again, not back down to the kitchen, but deeper into the prison. I ran with such speed, I would be nothing but a blur to any onlooker. I didn't know how I found my way so easily through the complex network of cells considering I'd only traveled through the basement in its entirety once, while following the leopard. But somehow, I didn't take a single wrong turn and it wasn't long before I found myself stepping out into the gardens of Jeramiah's atrium.

I barely took a moment to look over my surroundings. If there was anybody around, I didn't notice them. It was as if I had tunnel vision. I just felt the urge to keep running upward, right up to the highest level, and reach the desert above. I wasn't even sure what was calling me to do it, but I couldn't fight it.

Forsaking the elevators, I launched myself upward and leapt from level to level until I reached the highest point of the atrium—the glass-covered level just beneath the exit. I smashed through the glass and raced up the stairs toward the trapdoor. I forced it open and broke out into the desert night.

As I gazed around the shadowy dunes, it was as if

the cool wind blowing against my skin instilled within me another objective.

*I need to exit the boundary… and I need to reach a gate.*

*A gate.*

*Where is the nearest portal to the supernatural realm?*

I racked my brain, trying to recall the copy of Mona's map that I'd taken with me from The Shade and lost to the hunters back in Chile. I had studied that map intensely, but perhaps not intensely enough…

*Come on. Where is the nearest gate?*

I began running as I continued to think. A strong wind swept up around me, scattering sand in my eyes, but I barely felt the stinging. My focus was fixed on the boundary and my destination beyond. Now I was a member of the jinn's family, I could step outside of the invisible barrier, as other vampire residents like Jeramiah were able to.

I was only a few feet away from it when an invisible force punched me in the gut. Winded, I flew backward. I landed on the sand, but I didn't skip a beat. I shot to my feet and began running again.

"Benjamin!"

Nuriya's voice.

It'd never sounded so irritating to me as it did then.

The jinni appeared directly in front of me. My limbs froze. I was unable to take a single step forward or even budge an inch.

Aisha appeared by Nuriya's side, as well as the queen's lover, Bahir.

"I command you to let me free!" I growled. The anger that boiled up within me surprised even me.

Nuriya exchanged glances with Bahir and Aisha, then fixed her eyes on me.

"You've tipped the scales, Benjamin," she said quietly. "Now I must do what is best for you, my child."

I cursed the jinni. I was filled with an overwhelming desire to rip through her throat, if that was even possible. If I'd had control over my limbs, I would've tried.

She looked toward Bahir once again, and nodded.

Bahir looked directly at me and as he did, his upper body became as translucent as the mist swirling beneath him. The next thing I knew, he was hurtling toward me. A strong force hit my chest as he made contact with me, and then the most bizarre thing happened… the jinni's body melded right into me. I felt a strange, though not unwelcome, sense of warmth in my bones—something I'd never experienced as a vampire. The rage that had been welling up within me calmed and then vanished completely.

Nuriya returned control over my body. I staggered backward and, looking down, I realized just how coated I was with blood. My hands were caked with it, my clothes soaked as if I'd just fallen into a lake of the red substance.

The haze lifted, for the first time allowing the reality of what I'd just done to settle fully upon me. The aftertaste of human blood in my mouth, sweet as it was, now tasted like the most despicable thing on the planet. Wiping my mouth with the back of my hand, I spat on the ground, trying to rid my tongue of it in desperation. As though this act would somehow lessen the stabbing guilt. The crushing waves of dread.

"What just happened?" I panted, lowering myself on all fours and balling my hands into fists in the sand.

"You've had too much blood," Nuriya said. "The Elder is now strong enough to influence you in a way that he never was before... But I'm sure he wasn't counting on us assisting you. As subtle beings, we too can inhabit people. Bahir has entered inside you, and he is now attempting to smother the Elder's influence. That's why your mind has returned to you."

It took several moments for her words to sink in. *That jinni is inside me.* Two supernaturals within me, battling for control. Breathing heavily, I forced myself back to a standing position and stared at Nuriya.

"How long can Bahir remain with me?" I asked. I wasn't interested in much else other than how long I had before my mind was reclaimed.

"I'm unsure," Nuriya replied, gazing at me with

deep concern in her golden eyes. "Certainly, Bahir will not be able to stifle the Elder forever. This is only a temporary measure. He's just stalled the Elder calling you back to Cruor."

*Cruor. Of course. That's where the Elder wants me. That's why I was racking my brain as to where the nearest gate was. He's calling me back.*

Once I got there, that would be it for me. There'd be no coming back. And not just for me. I knew the consequences for the rest of the world, both human and supernatural, if the Elders were allowed to rise to power again.

If *I* allowed them to rise to power.

The Elder's influence had become so strong over me even without being physically present inside me. Once I arrived in Cruor, I assumed he'd be strong enough to enter me and use me as a vessel. He'd use me to nourish himself back to complete strength, and then gather new blood for the others to begin their recovery.

"No matter what happens," I said, trying to steady my breathing, "you can't let me reach Cruor."

Nuriya moved closer and gripped my arms. Her eyes blazed with determination. "I know, my child. We have to find a way out of this. Your future is with us, not those monsters."

As miserable as it would be, the thought of a life stuck with these jinn was almost appealing compared to what Cruor had in store for me.

*But even with this time Bahir has bought me, what the hell am I going to do now?*

As if Nuriya had read my thoughts, she said, "Perhaps you should go to visit Arron."

I stared at her. "Arron?"

"Yes," she replied. "He has great expertise in matters relating to the Elders—with Elders and Hawks being natural enemies, he made it his life's mission to know everything about those creatures in order to combat them. For the many, many years he's been alive, all the knowledge he has gained… some of it could be of use to us."

"So you're suggesting that the Hawk would actually want to help me?"

"It is in his interest as much as, if not more than,

yours that the Elders do not rise again. The Hawks are a weak shadow of their former selves. Just imagine what would happen if the Elders gained power and struck now—all of them would be obliterated. Arron would be horrified if he knew what the Elder had managed to do to you."

"That makes sense," I said, "but I still don't see why he would help me. Once he found out what I was carrying, what I have the potential of being used for—I don't see why he wouldn't just murder me on the spot. Finish me off, so that there was no chance of this catastrophe..."

Even as I said the words, a chill settled in at the base of my spine. What if that was the only way to stop them rising to power? Take myself out of the picture entirely... I shook aside the dark thought, and tried to focus on positive action. *There must be another way.*

"I don't doubt that murdering you would be the first thing that occurred to Arron," Nuriya replied. "You're the Elders' only link, their only hope of resuscitation. But you would not see Arron alone.

Although I have too many commitments here to come with you on such a journey, Aisha will come, and of course, Bahir will remain within you for as long as he possibly can."

"So you're suggesting that we actually go to Aviary?" I asked, raising a brow. I couldn't imagine how strange that would feel. The first, last and only time I'd been there had been as a newborn.

"Oh, no, of course not," Aisha butted in. "That would be an unnecessary risk with you as a vampire. We could pass through a gate and enter the supernatural world. Then I could leave you somewhere safe while I fetched Arron and brought him to see you."

I paused, thinking over the jinn's words. I wondered if Arron could hold answers that neither the jinn nor the oracle did—or rather, was willing to reveal. I knew that the jinn were on my side since I was one of them, but the oracle... Although she'd said that she'd seen my future set in stone, there was no way of knowing whether she might've been withholding some information from me. After her grim prediction, I could only hope it was true.

I looked toward Aisha, not thrilled that it was her I would have to be traveling with. But I was still too shaken to contemplate kicking up a fuss about it. I was just grateful that I had control of my mind again. I swallowed hard, then nodded.

I was dry of all ideas. I didn't know whether this Hawk could give us the answers we needed, but we had to keep moving. I could not remain stagnant.

"Where would you take me first?"

"To the nearest gate," Aisha said. "Once we're in the supernatural world, I think the best place for me to drop you off would be The Tavern. You could wait there while I fetched Arron."

"The Tavern," I muttered. It rang a bell. My parents had told me that they had stopped by a place called The Tavern on their mission to finish off the black witches.

"Yes," Aisha replied. "It's a small island, and it's kind of a haven for all species who have been rejected by their own kind—or for those who just choose to leave their homes and become wanderers. I'll be as fast as possible in fetching Arron, so I doubt you would be waiting long anyway."

Nuriya moved closer to me. Brushing her hands down my arms, she planted a kiss on top of my head. "And I will be here, waiting anxiously for your return, my child… Godspeed."

# Chapter 10: Sofia

Derek's hold around me tightened as Jeriad dipped beneath the clouds. We found ourselves staring down at what appeared to be an endless black desert. If this was really the country of jinn that we were hovering over, they clearly had a preference in habitat.

The dragons surrounding us came into view, carrying our companions, and soon we all touched down. Derek stood up on Jeriad's back, and, catching me by the waist, picked me up and dropped down on the sand before letting me stand on my own two feet.

We stepped back from the dragon, giving him space to transform. But to my surprise, he didn't.

"We will stay in our dragon forms for the time being," Jeriad explained.

"Now that we're here," Derek said, "I'd like you to shed some light on your plan."

"We are here to see an ancient family of jinn known as the Drizan. They are the most influential and feared of all the jinn clans. It was with them that we dragons once had an… exchange of favors, shall we say. I am of the belief that they will know about the Nasiris."

Jeriad stopped. Apparently that was all he was willing to reveal for the time being.

Our companions, now also debarked from their dragons, approached us. Rose stood on my left-hand side with Caleb. I caught her free hand and clutched it tight.

"All right," Derek said. "Lead us."

"I suggest we dragons surround you as we walk," Jeriad said.

The fire-breathers formed a circle around us as we

all moved forward on foot. As we trekked through the silky coal-black sand, the breeze was mild and pleasant and carried an odd, sweet aroma.

Jeriad stopped after a few hundred meters. I wasn't sure why. This patch of sand didn't look much different to any other... But then I noticed what Jeriad was staring down at. A medallion of sorts, with a diameter of five feet. It appeared to be forged of solid gold, and etched onto its surface was a symbol of a scorpion.

"We have arrived at the entrance to the jinn's lair," Jeriad informed us. "Now keep your distance."

We all stood back, including the other dragons, to give Jeriad space.

Raising his giant right hand, he brought it thumping down against the medallion. Once, twice, thrice.

And then he stepped back too, all of us waiting with bated breath.

Ten seconds later, a man appeared before us. At least, the top half of a man—his bottom half consisted of swirling red mist. If he had revealed his legs, I was certain that he would be taller than even Derek. His bare muscled chest was formidably built. His head was bald, his skin the color of deep ebony, and his heavy jaw looked out of proportion to the rest of his face. Thick eyebrows framed dark olive-green eyes—eyes that traveled along each of us before settling on Jeriad.

"Jeriad… What brings you to disturb the peace of the Drizan?" His voice was rich and deep like dripping honey. As he spoke, he revealed his thick teeth—every single one plated with gold. I was surprised that he recognized Jeriad instantly, since the dragon had said that it had been years since they had made contact.

"We do not intend to disturb you, Cyrus," Jeriad replied, eyeing the jinni steadily. "In fact, I have some information for you… Information that I believe might interest you greatly. About a family of jinn who have settled in the human realm."

Interest sparked in the jinni's eyes. He quirked a brow, his voice dropping to a hushed tone. "Could you be referring to the Nasiris by any chance?"

"Indeed, I am," Jeriad replied smoothly.

A sinister smile formed on the jinni's dark lips. "If you speak truth—and knowing that you are a creature of honor, I am sure that you do—then you and your companions are most welcome…"

There was a loud creak and the golden medallion lifted open like a trap door. The jinni gestured toward the gaping hole, beneath which was a jeweled staircase leading down to… who knew where. The jinni's eyes roamed the rest of us once again, a calm, unsettlingly friendly expression on his face. He gestured toward the staircase. "Please, be our guests."

# Chapter 11: Ben

Aisha made us vanish from the desert, and when we reappeared, it was at the edge of a massive lake.

"Where are we?" I asked.

"This is Lake Nasser," she replied, even as she began surveying our surroundings. Her eyes fixed on a small islet covered with tall shrubs and a few short trees, about a mile into the lake. She transported us there by magic and then began scanning the bushes around us, as if foraging for something. She pointed to my left. "Over there," she said, moving forward and beckoning for me to follow her.

She arrived in front of a particularly wide, clustered thicket. Stepping into the bushes revealed a gaping hole in the ground. A hole that looked familiar. I'd never visited this islet before, but I'd seen one of these gates before. As an infant, of course, and then as an adult—when I'd first discovered Kiev and Mona trying to break through the portal in that remote Hawaiian cavern. With the exception of the surroundings, this one was practically identical. I was looking down into the same endless, star-strewn abyss.

Without warning, Aisha nudged me—forcefully. I lost my balance and tripped. My stomach flipped as I lurched into a free fall, and I was surprised that all the blood I'd just consumed didn't immediately come gushing out of my mouth. I fell, twisting and turning in a spiral, my insides writhing painfully. I gasped with relief as I reached the end and went flying out.

I sat up, rubbing my head. I tried to open my eyes, but my sight was still hazy from the fall. I waited a few moments for my vision to clear.

We were in the middle of what appeared to be… another desert. Though this was unlike any that I'd seen on Earth. The sand was black as charcoal, and as I ran my finger through it, it was so smooth that it felt like I was touching silk. A half-moon lit up the night with surprising brilliance and the stars scattered in the sky, unhindered by any man-made pollution, blazed almost as brightly. The breeze that wafted past me was fragrant. It had a sweet scent, like honeysuckle.

Aisha had already passed through the gate and was hovering to my left.

"Where are we?" I asked.

"Never mind," she said. "This isn't our destination. We go to The Tavern now."

Before I could say another word, the sand disappeared beneath my feet and my vision blurred again. We arrived this time in the middle of a shadowy forest. Tall, thin trees surrounded us. It was almost pitch black, except for the few trickles of moonlight the canopy of leaves allowed through. In the distance, I could make out the sounds of some kind of settlement: a tide of voices, doors slamming, footsteps on stone, cutlery clattering.

I was about to open my mouth and ask where exactly we were now, but Aisha held a finger to her lips and shushed me. She slipped her hand into mine and pulled me forward. I let go of her hand in an instant, casting her a sharp sideways glance. Now that River was gone, I didn't want this girl getting any ideas—though I was sure that her impish mind was already full of them. The last thing I needed was any kind of distraction due to this jinni's stupid infatuation with me.

Aisha moved up ahead of me, apparently soured by my rejection of her hand-holding. I was happy to remain a few steps behind her.

It wasn't long before the edge of the forest came into view. We reached the border and gazed downward at a bustling town. Directly beneath us was a square with a small fountain in the center and surrounded by small makeshift cottages. Their thatched rooftops spread out for quite some distance, and beyond all of it was a high wall.

"This is The Tavern's town center," Aisha said, her eyes fixed on the odd assortment of crowds milling about below. She pointed toward a scruffy-looking building with a sign hanging outside: The Blue Tavern. "That's a pub and also a guesthouse. And I believe that's the safest place for you to wait while I'm searching for Arron."

"How long do you think you'll be?" I asked.

Aisha shrugged. "There is really no way of saying. I'm hoping that he will be fairly easy to find in Aviary, and I won't have to try to bribe—or more to the point, torture—the information out of somebody."

My eyes traveled back to the crowd.

"You said that all kinds of creatures inhabit this island?" I asked.

"A variety," Aisha said. "Not many live here permanently—most just come and go as they are on their travels... Let's go."

We moved down the slope leading from the forest to the square. Passing through the center of it, we headed straight for the pub. There were mostly vampires and werewolves surrounding us, though I also spotted an ogre and another bizarre-looking creature I'd never seen in my life. Its head was that of a woman, yet the rest of its short, stunted body was that of a feathery black bird. I thought at first that perhaps it was some kind of Hawk hybrid, but then Aisha followed my gaze and answered my curiosity.

"A harpy," she muttered. "Best not to look them in the eye."

*A harpy.* The creature caught my stare. Her sharp features contorted and her dark eyes narrowed as she glared at me. I looked away from the creature to notice how everyone in this square was gaping at Aisha as though she was an alien… which I guessed she kind of was. Most of them had likely never seen a jinni in their lives—confirming what Corrine had said about the creatures being practically legend even to many supernaturals.

Aisha's gaze was set firmly ahead as we reached the pub. She pushed open the creaky door and held it open for me to step inside. The place was crowded and shrouded with smoke. Dusty tapestries hung down the walls and as I looked around the room, I spotted mostly vampires. Werewolves sat on their hind legs, their forelegs resting on the table surface as they tucked messily into bowls of stew. I also spotted what appeared to be witches huddled together around one table, sipping from steaming cups. Then there was an ogre who occupied an entire table to himself, digging into what looked like a ten-course meal. Thankfully, I couldn't smell any humans.

Aisha led me to the bar counter where there was a line of one wolf and three vampires. She received many more stares, but she turned her back on all of them and fixed her focus on me. She looked quite unfazed by it all, perhaps even a little bored. I wondered how often she ventured outside of The Oasis—or if she ever did—but asking personal questions of her would only invite another unwanted advance.

Soon it was our turn. We moved up to the counter, on the other side of which was an apron-clad young male vampire with a closely shaved head. He rolled his sleeves up to his elbows as he gave us his attention.

Since we were standing right behind the counter, and there had been a crowd of people blocking his view when we entered, I realized that he hadn't yet seen the bottom of Aisha. He glanced over her with little more than appreciation for her exotic looks before turning to me. I eyed the strange-looking menu briefly, despite the fact that my body was capable of only ingesting a single substance—a substance that I had to avoid at all costs. From the looks of it, it was a true mishmash of drinks and food. It appeared that they really did strive to cater to all sorts. Some of the names of dishes I couldn't even pronounce.

"What can I get you?" the man asked.

"Nothing for me," Aisha answered before I could. "And nothing for this vampire either."

"Oh? Then what can I do for you?"

"My friend just needs somewhere to sit for a while," Aisha replied.

I was mildly surprised that she didn't slip a "boy-" in front of friend.

The man looked over our shoulders toward the crowded dining area. From where we stood, there wasn't a single empty table. He looked back at me. "If you can find somewhere to sit, you're welcome to stay."

"Also," Aisha said as the man was about to move on to serve the patron behind us, a burly-looking warlock, "might you have a spare room in your guest house tonight?"

I frowned. *Why is she asking that?*

"One moment," the man said. He reached beneath the counter and pulled out a black ledger. He paged through it and then nodded. "We do. One single room."

"That will be fine. I'd like to reserve that please. For tonight."

"Aisha, what—?" I began. She shot me a sharp look. Then, placing her right hand down on the counter, she left behind a heavy gold coin.

The man's eyes widened.

"I'm sure this will be payment enough?" she said sweetly.

The man nodded. "I'm sure," he said, a little breathless.

"Good," she said, a smile on her face. She caught my arm and pulled me away from the counter.

I glowered down at her. "What was that about? Why did you need to reserve a room?"

She ignored my question and cast her eyes about the room. "Over there," she said, pointing to our right. All the way over in one corner was the most empty table in the room. There was only one person sitting at it. A lone hooded figure. From where I stood, it was impossible to tell whether it was male or female.

Irritated by her evasiveness, I gripped Aisha's forearm and forced her to face me. "What is the room for?" I asked through gritted teeth.

She returned my glare. "It's for you," she hissed, jerking her arm out of my grasp. "I told you, I don't know exactly how long I'm going to be. I'm hoping I won't need more than a few hours, but in case I do need more... I just fixed you up with somewhere to sleep tonight. A thank you would be nice." She threw me a scowl. "Or maybe you would've preferred that I left you stranded in this grotty hole."

That wasn't the answer I had expected.

"Thank you," I said, my voice lower. I trusted from the offended look in her eyes that she wasn't lying to me.

We both looked back toward the almost empty table. Aisha jerked her head in its direction. "Go take a seat."

She turned her back on me and glided out of the pub.

I weaved my way through the maze of tables, keeping my gaze on the floor and avoiding eye contact. I neared the other side of the room and walked around the table, allowing me to see the face of the lone figure. She was a vampire, a young woman, her thin hands clasped around a glass of animal blood set on the table in front of her. Her raven-black hair hung beneath her hood in a bob that stopped beneath her ears, and bangs swept across one side of her forehead. Her features were slight, with high cheekbones sloping down to a narrow jawline and a small, pointed chin. She glanced up at me with large hazel eyes, deep-set and elongated. If I'd had to take a guess at her country of origin, I would have said Japan.

"May I take a seat?" I asked, clearing my throat.

She nodded, looking me over. "I'm not expecting anybody else."

I sat down. From this position I could better make out the room—at least when people weren't standing and blocking my view. The next table along was occupied by a group of four brown-cloaked vampires smoking pipes.

I hoped that Aisha wouldn't keep me waiting more than a few hours. Although she'd arranged a room for me, I didn't want to have to stay the whole night in this place. It wasn't like I'd be able to sleep. I just wanted to keep moving forward.

"Where are you from?" the young woman asked, interrupting my thoughts.

I stalled, wondering how best to answer her. Or if I should even answer her at all. She raised her glass to her small, round mouth and took a sip, eyeing me with mild curiosity.

"I'm a wanderer." I figured that was the easiest and shortest explanation I could give. And I realized with a grimace that it was actually accurate.

She nodded slowly, running a forefinger around the rim of her glass. "I am too," she said. "Do you travel alone or in a group?"

"Alone," I replied, now beginning to consider leaving this pub and going straight up to my room. If Aisha returned, she'd assume I'd gone upstairs. I really wasn't in the mood for talking with strangers.

"Hm," the young woman murmured. "So do I." She shifted her focus back to her glass.

She was quiet after that, neither asking me more questions nor offering more information about herself. Still, I decided to sit only five more minutes at the table before going up to my room. The noise and the smoke were beginning to get to my head. I craved the silence of solitude.

"Good night," I said as I stood up.

She nodded briefly in my direction.

My eyes traveled across the room, toward the

counter where the waiter stood. I needed to get the key to my room from him.

I was about to cross the pub to talk to him when the main door swung open, letting in a strong breeze and… a young human man. All at once, his scent surrounded me, exacerbated by the breeze. My hands clamped down around the edge of the table as my stomach knotted. I had Bahir within me delaying the Elder from taking over my mind, but I still felt the bloodlust just as badly. Even though my last feeding had only been hours ago.

The female vampire I'd been sharing the table with eyed me with a slight frown.

"Um… Are you all right?" she asked.

She twisted in her chair, following my gaze. The human—a man perhaps in his late twenties—had just made his way behind the counter. He picked up a broom and began to sweep up. Apparently he was a worker here.

"Are you newly turned?" the girl asked, pushing aside her now-empty glass and standing up.

"Something like that," I managed.

I wanted to bolt from this place, but there were only two exits that I could see—a staircase, and the main door. To reach both would mean traveling right past him, and I didn't want to risk that.

"Yeah," the girl murmured. "You don't want to go harming any humans here. Or anyone, for that matter. I don't know if you've been to The Tavern before—I'm guessing you haven't if you're newly turned. The laws here are strict. Very strict. You could be sentenced to execution even for getting into a fight here."

I glanced at her, disbelieving.

"It's the only way they can maintain peace with such a myriad of conflicting species all milling about in one area."

I guessed it made sense.

I looked back toward the counter, hoping for any sign of the human leaving. He was only showing signs of staying as he put down the broom and picked up a mop before cleaning the floor in front of the bar.

I started to panic as my vision began to shroud again. I guessed that it would be a matter of seconds now before—

"Do you have a room in this place?" the hazel-eyed girl asked, walking around me and standing directly in front of me.

"Yes," I breathed, grateful for her distraction. My eyes demisted a little, my vision becoming clearer at her interruption. "I'm booked to stay in one of the rooms, but I need the key…"

"Ah." She glanced back over at the counter. "Well, I've finished my drink. I don't mind asking the guy for your key. Just keep yourself in this corner."

Even that felt like a gargantuan task. But I couldn't have been more appreciative for her offer of help in that moment.

"That would be… great," I panted. "And if you could hurry…"

She gave me a small, knowing smile, and then dashed off. She arrived behind the counter, spoke to the vampire waiter and gestured back toward me.

The man glanced my way before opening up a cabinet and pulling down a key, which he handed the young woman. She swept back across the room toward me, deftly snaking around the tables.

"Thank you," I said as she handed me the key.

Now I just had to figure out how to get up the staircase and also hope that once I was up there, my room would be far away enough from the ground floor for the smell to not bother me so much.

"I'm, uh, retiring to bed now anyway, if you're headed for the stairs..." the girl said.

She walked by my side, the side that was closer to the human, as we left the table. I rushed toward the staircase and ran up it. Her standing so close to me helped. I felt a twinge in my chest as I thought of River, how much I'd come to rely on her to act as my boundary during the time we spent together. As I climbed the staircase with the girl, I imagined where River would be now. In The Shade, I hoped. I wondered how she had taken waking up to find me gone. How she was coping. How her family was adjusting to the island. Whether they would all stay there. Whether I might ever see River again...

"I'm Julie, by the way," the girl said.

She looked at me as though she was expecting me

to offer my name. I didn't. I was grateful to her for helping me out of that predicament, but I wasn't here to make friends.

"Your room is sixty-seven," she said as we continued up the winding staircase and reached level six. I jumped up four steps at a time, quickening my arrival at my level.

I looked back at her. "Thank you again."

She shrugged. "No problem. I'll maybe see you around… Or not."

*Or not* would be a realistic expectation.

# Chapter 12: Ben

Julie disappeared up the staircase while I entered a long, wide corridor that spanned the sixth level. I was shocked at the size of the place. From outside in the square where Aisha and I had first entered, the Blue Tavern had looked like a narrow building. Now I could see that its accommodation space sprawled out across the floors of the attached buildings on either side of the pub.

At least it was big enough for the scent of human blood downstairs to not bother me so much, especially as I walked further and further down the corridor. I arrived outside room sixty-seven, pushed in the key and opened the door. I stepped into a small, basic room. There was a single bed in one corner, and a tiny bathroom attached. There was no window in this room either, and the carpets looked worn. The sheets and pillow also looked like they had seen better days, but the place seemed clean at least. Not that it mattered much. I was just glad to be on my own, away from the human and the crowds.

I stepped into the bathroom and washed my face. I glanced at myself in the mirror, relieved to see that my eyes were still green.

*Don't leave me yet, Bahir.*

I felt like a walking time bomb. Not even the jinn seemed to have much of an idea as to how long Bahir could remain within me. And once he left, there'd be nothing stopping me from…

I caught myself. I needed to stop dwelling on worst-case scenarios. I just needed to hope that Aisha was fast in bringing Arron to me.

I breathed out slowly, trying to calm my racing

mind.

I thought more about Arron. What it would be like meeting him for the first time since I was a newborn. I still found it hard to believe that he could be of help to us. I hoped that Nuriya had been right in assuming that he would want to do all he could to help us stop the Elders' plan.

I lay on the bed and stared up at the ceiling for the next few hours, mulling over the meeting with Arron in my mind, and what solution he could possibly suggest. If he had any suggestions at all. I found myself sick of all the speculating and eventually closed my eyes.

Then my stomach lurched.

Human blood.

I could smell it again. Not a distant, diluted hint. It was strong. Too strong. As though a human was walking right by my room.

I leapt from the bed and backed up against the wall, trying not to breathe in too much of the scent.

*Where is it coming from?*

I wondered if it might be that same cleaning man

from downstairs, now come upstairs to do his work. I crept toward the door, and clutched the handle. What if he was standing right outside? No barrier between my fangs and his throat whatsoever... Just a few steps.

I groaned in frustration and slammed my fists against the wall.

The scent was driving me insane. As much as I couldn't risk going outside, I also knew I couldn't remain here in this confined room, with this tantalizing aroma invading my nostrils.

If I waited much longer, I didn't trust myself to not burst outside of the room and hunt down the human. I had to get out of here while my vision was still clear.

I twisted the door handle and poked my head out into the corridor. It was empty, to my relief. I tried to place exactly where the scent was coming from— somewhere to my left, perhaps a few doors along? I looked to my right. At the end of the long corridor was another staircase. Grabbing the key to the room, I darted out and sped toward it. I climbed the stairs, passing level seven, eight, nine, and stopping at what appeared to be the highest floor—ten. I stopped at a window in the corridor and pushed it wide open. From here, I had a view of the sea over the high wall that surrounded this island.

The blustery wind blew through the window, surrounding me. It helped to soothe my senses, diluting the atmosphere with a salty scent. The knots in my stomach loosened. I planted my arms on the windowsill and poked my head out of the window, relishing the cool breeze ruffling my hair. This was better. Much better.

A door clicked behind me, followed by the sound of a familiar female voice. "You again?"

I turned around to see Julie standing half in, half out of Room 107. A couple of damp towels hung over one arm and she had changed into a dark green nightgown. I felt awkward as I looked at her.

"Yeah," I muttered. "I think a human moved into the room right next to me or something…"

"Oh," she said. "Wow, you really must be newly turned."

I nodded stiffly.

"So you're just going to stand there all night?" she asked.

Truth be told, I hadn't thought past the next hour. For all I knew, Aisha could return before then with Arron.

"Perhaps," I murmured vaguely.

Julie shrugged, then stepped out of the room. She passed by me and headed down the stairs.

When she returned a few minutes later, her arm empty of the towels, I was still standing in the same spot. She passed by me again and headed toward her door, but before entering, she hesitated.

"I remember when I was newly turned," she commented. "It was really tough... I don't mind swapping rooms with you if it could help prevent a murder..." She arched a brow in question. "I haven't unpacked yet, so it doesn't make a lot of difference to me."

I looked at her, weighing her words and wondering whether there was any point in accepting her offer if Aisha was going to return soon... Still, I didn't have any guarantee that the jinni would be fast. I thought it wiser to accept. If the corridors got busier, I'd be thankful for a private room.

"If you don't mind," I said. "I would be grateful."

She moved back into her room and reappeared a few moments later carrying a large brown shoulder bag. She wore the black cloak she'd had on earlier.

She handed me her key, and I gave her mine.

"Well, goodbye... again." She looked amused as she left the corridor and padded down the staircase.

Now that I had calmed down, I felt that it was safe for me to step away from the window. I entered my new room. It was no larger than the one I'd left on level six, and came with the same basic amenities—a single bed and a small bathroom attached. Although this one had a window, to my pleasant surprise. I pushed it open. Now I wouldn't even need to stand in the corridor when I wanted fresh air. The more I kept to myself, the better.

I sat on the bed and leaned against the wall, staring out of the window at the glistening sea beyond. The moon still had full reign over the sky, but I guessed it would only be a few hours before the first signs of day showed on the horizon.

I found myself wondering whether the island was protected by a spell of night. And if it wasn't, I wondered what most vampires did to cope during the day, especially those who lived here full time. I guessed that was why this place came so alive at night.

I hadn't thought that I would stand a chance of drifting off to sleep that night, and while what I drifted off into could hardly be called sleep—my senses were still alert—it was a far more comfortable state than being awake. I managed to find some semblance of peace amidst the storm.

A peace that was broken an hour later when the window above me blasted open.

# Chapter 13: Ben

Splinters of glass rained down on me. I leapt to my feet and found myself face to face with a tall, broad-shouldered vampire I'd never seen in my life. His hair was short, fine and black. A mask covered the upper portion of his face, but from the structure of his cheekbones and the tone of his skin, he appeared to be of Asian descent.

His brown eyes widened behind his mask and he looked just as shocked to see me as I felt to see him. He quickly recovered, however, and lurched forward, motioning to grab my neck. My leg shot out and I kicked him hard in the gut, sending him shooting backward and colliding with the wall.

He crumpled to the floor, but was again fast to regain composure. Reaching beneath his cloak, he slid out a sharp wooden stake.

"Where's Ms. Duan?" he hissed.

*Ms. Duan? Is he looking for Julie?*

"Who are you?" I glowered at him.

His grip on the stake tightened, and he moved closer to me. "Where is the woman?" he said in a low, threatening voice.

I had not the slightest clue as to why this man had just broken through the window, and what he wanted with Julie—assuming she was Ms. Duan. I wasn't sure how he knew that Julie had booked this room, but whoever he was, he didn't exactly give me the impression that he was a friend of hers.

It would have been easy to just tell him we'd swapped rooms and she was now in Room 67. But, although the last thing I needed was any kind of trouble, I wasn't about to tell him where the young woman was staying. Not after the help she'd offered me. For all I knew, he could be here to murder her. He'd certainly come equipped with the means to do so...

Eyeing the tip of the stake this vampire had pointed at me, I squared my shoulders and broadened my stance, gearing up to disarm him.

"I don't know who Ms. Duan is," I said through gritted teeth. "But I do know that you have exactly thirty seconds to climb back out of that window."

He lunged forward with the stake. I ducked, narrowly missing being gouged, and swept a leg beneath his feet, knocking him to the floor. I motioned to grab his weapon, but he was too fast. His arm shot out and he swept it from the floor a split second before my hand closed around it. Still lying on his back, he swung it in front of him, pointing it upward and forcing me backward as he threatened my midriff. Grabbing a particularly sharp shard of glass from the windowsill and ignoring the way its edges cut into my palms, I was about to launch myself at him when a second vampire slid through the window.

He too wore a mask, though, as with his companion, it didn't hide his alarm on seeing me. Enough of his face was visible for me to see that he too hailed from the Orient. He slid out a stake from beneath his own cloak and brandished it at me.

I was hoping to avoid killing someone here, but as he plunged the stake toward my heart, it was clear that they would have no qualms about murdering me… which meant I had to give up my own qualms.

I hurled the shard of glass toward his head like a dagger. He yelped and staggered back as the glass dug into his right cheek.

The first vampire scrambled up from the floor where I'd knocked him. Leaping behind him, I held him in a choke and twisted his neck until it snapped. He sank to the floor, paralyzed.

That left me with one vampire to deal with. He'd yanked the glass from his cheek—which was now healing fast—and launched at me once more, his stake aimed at my heart. I dodged, causing him to miss my chest, but not the edge of my shoulder. The stake's sharp tip sliced a gash in my bicep.

Angered, I leapt upward and grabbed hold of one of the wooden beams in the ceiling. My right leg hurtled toward the vampire and I kicked his head against the wall. His stake thudded to the floor. I leapt back down and wrestled him into submission beneath me. Then, extending my claws, with one swift motion I dug my right hand deep into his chest and tore through his heart.

Panting, I stood up and gazed around the wrecked, blood-splattered guest room. I swore beneath my breath before rushing to the bathroom. I rinsed off the blood from my body as best as I could before covering myself with my cloak. It was a good thing that I was wearing mostly dark clothes.

Someone in this guesthouse was bound to have heard all that—I wouldn't have been surprised if the struggle was audible to supernatural ears even from down in the noisy bar. I stepped out of the room into the thankfully still-empty corridor and shut the door behind me. I found myself scanning the ceiling and walls instinctively for CCTV cameras before reminding myself that I wasn't on Earth. Perhaps they had some other kind of surveillance system that wasn't detectable to me. Whatever the case, there was only one thing I could think to do now.

I raced down the stairs to the sixth level and swept along the corridor until I stood outside Room 67. I heard soft breathing through the door. It sounded like Julie was asleep. I rapped against the door, loudly, but not loudly enough to sound desperate to neighbors on either side—or so I hoped.

A mattress creaked and soft footsteps moved toward the door. The handle turned and Julie appeared in the doorway. Her cropped black hair was tousled, and she was rubbing sleep away from her eyes as she looked at me, squinting from the corridor lighting.

Her lips parted to exclaim in surprise, but before she could, I clamped a palm over her mouth and pushed her back through the door. I pulled it shut behind me.

"What are you doing?" she gasped as I let go of her. She backed up against the wall, extending her claws.

"Is your surname Duan?"

She froze. "H-How do you know that?"

"Two men just broke into your room," I said in a voice barely louder than a breath. "They were looking for a *Ms. Duan.*"

Julie's jaw dropped. "Two men?" she asked in a choked voice. Her breathing grew fast and uneven. "Wh-What did they look like?"

I described their appearance as best as I could from what I'd seen around their masks.

"Oh, God." She clasped a thin hand over her mouth. "They're after me."

"Who is after you?"

"What happened? Where are they now?"

"One paralyzed, one dead on the floor of your room."

"Oh, no. No. No. No. I-I have to leave," she stammered. She appeared to be in a state of shock as she grabbed her shoulder bag and began stuffing into it the few personal possessions she had placed on the mantelpiece and bedside table. She dashed into the bathroom and when she came back out, her face was stricken with terror. "I have to leave," she repeated. "And you have to leave, too. You have no idea of the punishment The Tavern would deal you for slaughtering a person. We both have to get out of here!"

I stared at her. "Where to?"

"I-I don't know, but we must flee this island before someone discovers them." Her lips quivered, her voice was close to cracking.

I would have been surprised if nobody had gone to investigate already. Unless guests of the Blue Tavern were used to banging coming from rooms... but the noise we'd made would have been hard to pass off as even wild vampire lovemaking.

Still wearing her nightdress, Julie grabbed her cloak from the back of the door before flinging on her shoulder bag.

"Julie, who were those people?"

She barged past me toward the door and stopped just as she reached it. Her hand rested on the handle. Her back heaved as she drew in a deep, rasping breath.

"I have a boat that I used to get here," she whispered, ignoring my question. "It's moored in The Tavern's harbor. I'm going to run straight there now, and try to get far away before dawn breaks." She turned around to face me, a look of worry in her eyes. "I suggest that you do the same in your boat."

My mind worked quickly. I didn't have a boat, of course. But if I followed Julie to the harbor, I would have to hope that I could find a suitable one. Then I would have to wait off The Tavern's shore in safety until Aisha returned. I had the gold band around my wrist so I wasn't too concerned about her finding me. I'd touch the snake's head and that should summon her to me.

"Okay," I breathed, seeing that Julie wasn't going to answer my question—at least not now. "Let's go."

She pulled the door open and we both poked out our heads, looking right and left, scanning the length of the corridor. I was relieved to see that it was still empty. Julie darted left, toward the nearest staircase to us, and I followed quickly behind her. We flew down the stairs, level after level, as silently as we could, and arrived on the ground floor. We approached the door that led into the pub and peered through the glass. The eatery was still packed with people—no less packed than when we'd left it, in fact. We pushed open the door, and, keeping our heads down, tried to be as inconspicuous as possible as we slipped into the crowd and made our way toward the exit. We stepped out into the early morning air.

Julie pulled her hood lower down her face and took a right. She was short and slight of build, able to squeeze through narrow gaps in crowds in a way I couldn't, so I had to make a concerted effort to not lose sight of her as she scrambled forward. I didn't take in much of my surroundings as I followed the vampire. I just kept my eyes focused on her back.

Soon we had left The Tavern's town center and entered a much quieter area. We hurried along cobbled stone streets, until Julie raced down a flight of stairs and stopped at the bottom, in front of a heavy wooden door. An ogre was slumped in a chair beside it, his eyes closed, his head lolling onto his chest. Julie shot me a sharp glance and placed a finger over her lips.

She crept up to the door and slid open the bolts. They were large and heavy and, no matter how quiet she tried to be, the metal ended up making an uncomfortable amount of noise. But thankfully—and perhaps predictably—the ogre slept through it. Julie creaked the door open just wide enough for the two of us to slip through, then closed it again behind us.

We emerged on the beach that lined the other side of the high wall surrounding The Tavern.

Julie didn't miss a beat. She sprinted toward a port in the distance, a network of wooden platforms surrounded by a myriad of boats and ships.

Julie kicked up a storm of sand as she tore along the beach. Catching up with her, I ran by her side. Her eyes were fixed forward, still wide with terror.

"Are you going to tell me who those men were?" I asked, irritated at the lack of an answer considering they had just attempted to murder me.

"I just need to… get to my boat," she panted.

Although impatient for answers, I didn't press her. We traveled along the maze of wooden platforms that extended into the sea and connected each of the ships. It was our good luck that I didn't spot anyone else here at this time of the morning. I had to hope that it would stay that way while I found a vessel to steal for myself.

Julie halted in front of a small boat whose deck was covered entirely by a curved wooden shelter. She leapt up onto the deck's railing and looked down at me. "This is my boat," she said. "I suggest you hurry up and find yours."

"Julie—" I began, exasperated.

She shook her head. "It doesn't matter to you who those men were. All you need to know is that you have to get out of here. Go to your boat and just... get lost."

With that, she leapt from the railing down onto her deck and disappeared from sight.

I exhaled in frustration. I cast my eyes around the harbor.

*I'm going to have to steal another boat.*

Surrounding Julie's boat were mostly large ships, none of which would be suitable for me. I raced through the harbor, weaving in and out of vessels until I came across a boat that looked more suitable for my purposes. It was even smaller than Julie's, and I guessed that it belonged to a vampire because it also had a wide covering. Feeling guilty that I was thieving yet again, I climbed aboard and headed to the small compartment at the front that I could only assume was a control room.

Stepping inside, I felt confused. This was unlike any boat I had ever traveled in. What I had thought was a compartment was more like a long screen, separating the back of the boat from the front. There was no wall in front of me. The compartment was wide open, giving a full view over the bow of the boat. A wide cushioned seat was fixed a few feet in front of the door I'd just stepped through, and in front of that was some kind of metal stand upon which rested two thick ropes. The ropes, secured in place by iron clamps, trailed down the front of the vessel and extended into the water. I thought perhaps this was a way of anchoring the boat, so I followed the ropes to the edge and looked down into the sea.

*Not exactly an anchor.*

I found myself staring down at two black shadows beneath the water. Some kind of sharks. Their shiny fins poked above the surface. The ropes bound the creatures like… reins. I cast my eyes around the other boats and spotted the same type of sturdy reins dipping down into the ocean, each tied to a variety of sharks and other smaller creatures—a species of dolphin.

My eyes traveled back to the sharks that were tethered to my boat, and I looked around the deck once more, just to be sure that there was no kind of engine. Heck, there weren't even sails on this boat.

I'd learned to navigate a submarine, and found it fairly intuitive to navigate a boat—but a boat drawn by sharks? How exactly would I communicate to them which way to go? Perhaps it was a bit like riding a horse, something I'd never done in my life.

Brushing aside my apprehension, I took a seat in front of the reins and slowly unraveled them from the stand. I clutched them tightly and tugged a little, feeling the resistance of the sharks. I experimented tugging with different levels of pressure, but found that the sharks only bolted forward once I tugged hard.

Their speed caught me by surprise. I found myself forced back in the seat. They swam straight ahead, and while I still wasn't sure how to steer them, straight ahead was good enough for now.

I looked back toward the shadowy harbor as the sharks pulled me away. A wave of déjà vu washed over me as I recalled the last time I had stolen a boat. I'd been with River. She'd taken it upon herself to scare off the security guards while I navigated. I remembered the shaken look on her face as she'd put down the gun…

"Help!"

A strained call. Julie's voice.

It came from somewhere behind me, to my right. I spun around to see her standing on the bow of her boat, soaking wet with her arms outstretched, waving frantically.

*What in the world?*

I tugged on the sharks and managed to pull them to a stop. With a lot of trial and error, I steered the animals around and headed toward Julie's boat.

"What?" I called in a hushed tone as I neared her.

She pointed down at the water. It was stained with blood. The corpses of two sharks bobbed near the surface.

"They came here to my boat first," she breathed. "They destroyed the cabin area, plundered my supplies, chopped the reins to bits, a-and slaughtered my animals." Tears of panic lined the corners of her eyes.

Swallowing hard, I moved my boat closer. Steadying herself, she took a leap, and landed shakily on the deck.

"We need to get far, far away from here!" she whispered.

Tugging on the reins again, I tried to steer the sharks again. Noticing my inexperience, Julie gripped the reins and pulled them from my hands, taking control of them herself. She guided them toward the open sea with practiced ease.

As we skidded through the waves, Julie cast a glance my way. "I-I'm sorry," she said, her voice low but a little steadier. "I hate to intrude like this. I won't be a burden. You can drop me off wherever you're headed and I'll find my way from there."

*I highly doubt you want to go wherever I'm headed.*

# Chapter 14: Ben

Wrapping the reins around her wrists, Julie took a seat on the chair.

I remained half-glaring, half-watching her closely until, finally, she threw me a bone.

"Those men," she said. "They meant to kidnap me tonight."

"Why? Who were they?"

She drew in a deep breath. "They are allies of my father."

That was the last answer on earth I'd expected to

hear.

"Why would your father want to kidnap you?"

She smiled bitterly. "Fair question... One that wouldn't surprise you if you knew anything about the Taihang coven."

I raised a brow.

She let out a sigh.

"It's a coven that used to inhabit the Taihang Mountains. In China."

So the Elders had infiltrated China too. I doubted my parents knew about that—at least they'd never mentioned it to me. India, China, where else?

"My father was—and still is—its leader," she continued. "After the demise of the Elders, he led us into this supernatural world where we all became full-time wanderers. Or perhaps pirates would be a better term. We—or I should say they—have a big ship that they live on—mostly at sea, though sometimes they stop at a port if the atmosphere isn't too hostile. I... I escaped."

"Why did you escape?"

She turned her gaze away from me and set it

straight ahead on the ocean.

"Because my father is a tyrant." She bit down hard on her lower lip. "My mother died a year ago, and something snapped in him. He was always an authoritarian, but now he rules our coven with an iron fist. And me..." She paused. "He was forcing me into a marriage I was desperately unhappy with."

*Great. So I've got some kind of runaway princess on my hands.*

"So you're Chinese?" I said.

"My mother is... was... Japanese. But my father's birthplace is China."

I hadn't been too far off in guessing her roots.

"And you came to The Tavern because you thought you would be safe there, I assume," I said.

"Yes," she replied. "I hoped I could keep my head down and live there inconspicuously. But I was stupid to think that my father wouldn't find me. Those guys who broke in, I'm sure that they were my father's two right-hand men... Ling and Zhao." She seemed to sense my tension. "Look, as I said, I really don't want to be a burden. You can drop me off wherever you're planning to go." She looked around the boat. "Where did you get a boat like this?" she wondered. "I noticed you weren't exactly proficient in leading your sharks…"

*That's one way to put it.*

I didn't see much of a reason to lie. This girl seemed harmless enough and clearly had more than enough of her own problems.

"I stole it," I said bluntly.

She frowned. "Oh. So you don't actually own a boat?"

"No."

"You told me that you travel alone, so then how did you get to The Tavern? And what is your name, if you don't mind me asking?"

"My name is Benjamin. I got to The Tavern with… someone else's help."

"And where do you plan to go now?"

"Just far away enough from The Tavern to be safe. And then I plan to float on the water until my companion returns for me."

"Oh. So your companion has a boat?"

"Not exactly… My companion is a jinni."

"A jinni?" Her eyes bulged. "Oh, my goodness. I never even knew there was such a thing."

"Well… there is. She'll appear on this deck. I expect her to find me within a few hours. And when she does come for me, you can have this boat and go wherever you want."

Julie paused. "Where do you come from, Benjamin?"

*From the depths of hell,* I thought grimly to myself, but replied, "Egypt."

"You're not Egyptian though."

"No." I heaved a sigh. "Originally, I'm from an island in the Pacific Ocean."

I would have been stupid to not expect her to instantly respond with: "You mean The Shade?"

The Shade was a legend to almost all vampires. That much my parents had told me.

"Yes," I said heavily. "The Shade is my home."

"Then why on earth did you come here? Who in their right mind would leave that island?"

I wasn't exactly in the mood to dig up my whole

horror story. But seeing that there wasn't much else to do while I waited for Aisha to return, I found myself giving Julie a brief history. I could see from the look on her face that much of my story was blowing her mind. She had apparently grown up in a coven of vampires, but I supposed that she had been fairly isolated from the rest of the world in those Chinese mountains. And then when she'd arrived in the supernatural world, she appeared to have been living in her parents' shadow, or more specifically, her jerk of a father's.

Inevitably, my recount also involved revealing that I was a Novak, and Prince of the island, at which point she looked at me with awe.

As hours passed, and Aisha still had not returned, I came to the brink of telling Julie the real reason why I had entered the supernatural world. I hesitated, wondering whether I really wanted to go down that rabbit hole with her. In the end, I did. Partly to pass the time, and partly because I'd already told her the rest of my story. I didn't see much point in holding back the last piece.

She gaped at me. "Imprinted by an Elder. That's… horrifying. W-What are you going to do?"

I shrugged. "That's what I'm here to figure out. Aisha, my jinni companion, has gone to find Arron. And I'm expecting her back anytime now."

I blew out in frustration. I wished I had a watch so that I could keep track of the time. Then again, perhaps I should have been grateful that I didn't have one. Watching the minutes go by might have just made me more tense.

"So you're basically on your own here, except for the jinni who is helping you?" Julie asked.

"Yes," I replied. "And of course I have Bahir who's still within me… somewhere."

Julie's eyes were filled with concern. She chewed on her lower lip. "What… What would happen if you weren't successful in breaking the bond the Elder has with you?" she asked.

I looked at her. It should've been obvious to her what would happen. "I can't afford to think about not being successful."

# CHAPTER 15: BEN

The sun had already risen by the time Aisha finally returned. I was infinitely grateful that the boat had a wide covering over it, allowing us to remain untouched by the sun's rays. I breathed out in relief as the jinni appeared on the deck. But a second later, when it registered that she was alone, alarm gripped me.

I shot to my feet. "Where is he?"

Aisha looked a little flustered, her hair disheveled. She glanced curiously at Julie, who was gaping back at her, before fixing her focus on me.

"I found him," she said.

The knot in my stomach loosened a little. "Then where is he? And what took you so long?"

"It took me a while to find him. Aviary's city, where he used to live, has been abandoned since the war, and they shifted to an entirely different part of their country… It just took me a while to locate it. As for Arron, I left him on a nearby islet. I think it will be better to talk there than on this small boat… But, Benjamin, what happened to you? I fixed you up with a room, so why are you waiting out here?"

I groaned internally before outlining what had just happened. Aisha looked taken aback, her eyes falling once more on Julie.

Catching Julie's eye, I gestured to the boat. "Well, this is all yours now."

I expected her to look relieved, but strangely she didn't. She looked… torn. Conflicted. Perhaps even a little disappointed.

"Um, Benjamin… if I'm honest with you, and with myself, I don't really have anywhere else to go now that I've been kicked out of The Tavern. I guess I could try to find some neutral land where I could stay, but... I've kind of got a lot of free time on my hands. It sounds like you've got a huge load on your plate, and doing this all alone..." She paused, clasping her hands together. Her eyes darted to the floor. "If everything you've said about the Elders' plan to rise to power through you is true, your success or failure in this mission will determine the safety of all realms... I mean, it seems that this isn't just your fight. This is a fight that we all have a stake in... if you'll excuse the pun."

I stared down at the vampire, wondering exactly what she was suggesting.

"It doesn't seem right that you should go through this so alone. I have nothing better to do and I couldn't think of a better use of my time than this... I'm willing to help you in whatever small way I can."

It was of course true what she said, that the outcome of this mission would affect every realm in existence, but it didn't dampen the strong desire I had to go through this alone and not bring anyone along with me. Besides, I had no idea how her accompanying me would even be of use.

"I appreciate that, Julie," I said. She clearly had guts to offer to come with me after everything I'd told her about my situation. "But I honestly don't see how you could be of help."

To my surprise, Aisha spoke up. "Actually, Ben," she said, looking thoughtfully at Julie, "if this girl is really willing to come along, having a second vampire might just come in handy."

I was taken aback. After all Aisha's jealousy and possessiveness over me with River, I'd expected her to treat every female I happened to stand within a few feet of the same way.

Now she was recommending that we bring a second female into our fold—and a vampire, at that.

"How exactly?" I asked.

"I'm not sure," the jinni replied. "We still don't know what this journey holds for us, but I just have a feeling—call it an instinct—that we might be better off bringing her."

I looked back at Julie, still unconvinced. "Look," I

said to the vampire, "you don't need to do this, and you will regret this decision. I'm grateful for the help you offered me so far, and that has been more than enough to set me on my way. It seems to me like your main reason for wanting to join us is that you have nothing else to do."

Julie looked slightly offended. "It's true that I'm on the run with nowhere to go... but that doesn't change the fact that I don't think it's right that you go through this so alone. I've been in the supernatural world for a long time. I'm sure I have some knowledge or could offer some assistance that could help you along the way."

Aisha touched my forearm. "This girl is offering to come, Ben. I suggest you just let her. She seems to be quite aware of the risks... But whatever you decide, hurry up. Arron is waiting for us."

I'd been going to refuse Julie outright before Aisha butted in and recommended that I let her come. Now, I felt conflicted. It didn't seem wise to ignore the jinni's words—especially when it appeared that she had no hidden motive and was simply giving advice on what she thought was best. That was rare behavior from what I had observed of Aisha since I'd met her.

I looked reluctantly back at the vampire. She might get cold feet soon enough anyway—I wouldn't be surprised if it happened directly after our meeting with Arron, who, considering my luck, would probably deliver some more grim news.

I also had a thought at the back of my mind that perhaps, just perhaps, stumbling across Julie was meant to happen. Perhaps Julie really could be of use to us at some point during this uncharted journey.

The vampire was right that I needed all the help I could get. Though I still wasn't sold, I found myself agreeing. "Okay. You can come with us. But you do realize it means leaving behind this boat? So you'd really better be sure about this decision."

Julie eyed the boat, then clutched her shoulder bag closer to her. She nodded, swallowing hard. "I'd like to come with you. It feels like the right thing to do… And I guess I will still have the option to pull out. I might lose this boat, but perhaps Aisha could drop me off somewhere…"

"All right, enough talk," Aisha said briskly. "She's made up her mind. Let's go to Arron." The jinni clutched my arm and then reached for Julie's before all three of us vanished in a veil of mist.

# Chapter 16: Ben

Aisha made us reappear on an islet populated by small fruit trees and wild bushes. Now that we were away from the covering of the boat, I expected the blinding sun to begin digging into my skin as we stood out in the open, but Aisha had already taken care of that for us. The top of a wide parasol hung midair above our heads, keeping the worst of the sun away. There were definitely perks to traveling with a jinni.

I looked around the bumpy landscape, then frowned. "So… where is Arron?"

Aisha beckoned for the two of us to follow her as she moved forward. She led us across the islet, through thickets of bushes, and as we neared a small tree, I spotted a figure that could only have been Arron. Sitting on the ground, his back turned, he appeared to be tied to the tree. He must've heard the crunching of twigs beneath our feet as we approached. He craned his neck around to reveal his sharp beaked face. His gray eyes widened as he stared up at me.

I looked him over with silent contempt. This was the man who had kept me captive as a newborn. I of course had no memories of him from my visit to Aviary. I only knew what he looked like from the vision the jinn had given me. Arron looked a lot more bedraggled now than he had then. His hair was thinner and practically white. His face looked lined and worn. And as he sat there—tied to the tree by some kind of invisible rope—I realized that he had lost an entire arm and wing. This must've been the injury he'd incurred during the battle with the Elders. He was lucky to even be alive after that war.

"Ben," Aisha said, "meet Arron. I have already

explained to him why we are here, and why I kidnapped him from Aviary."

Arron grimaced.

Aisha nudged his head with her hand. "So, tell us what you know, Hawk," she said, looking down at him expectantly.

Arron's sharp eyes met mine. I still couldn't get over how strange it was to be seeing him in the flesh. This legend of a Hawk, reduced to a weak victim. It appeared that Aisha had made his body rigid because he wasn't even attempting to move. The only movement he made was turning his head.

"Benjamin Novak," he said slowly. His baritone voice was nasal. "I didn't expect that we would meet again… You look just like your father."

Aisha unceremoniously prodded him again. "We don't have all day," she said.

I bent down on the ground, so that my face was level with his. "You know what would happen if the Elders were allowed to rise to power again," I said. "You know better than anyone. So I suggest that you be as helpful as possible. Aisha has told you about the situation, and you know the Elders' plan for resurgence. What do you have to say?"

The look in Arron's eyes was that of deep dislike. He paused, then said, "If the greater good is really what interests you, Benjamin, then you would simply remove yourself as a risk."

His tone bordered on patronizing.

My eyes narrowed on him. "What are you saying exactly?"

"I'm saying that you are the only hope for the Elders right now. They are bankrupt of blood and vessels, and even if they had vessels, they have become too weak to inhabit them."

"What would be the use of calling Ben back to Cruor then, if none could actually inhabit him?" Aisha asked, looking dubious.

Arron continued to address me. "You, Benjamin, are the only exception. Because of the unique bond you have with Basilius, if you came within his proximity, he could live within you and use you to not only recover himself, but also set the ball rolling for the others. In other words, you are their only hope.

Hence, you and you alone will be responsible for the Elders' coming to power. If you didn't exist, they would remain the dormant spirits that they are now. That's why I say, if you really care about the greater good… then you would eliminate yourself from the equation."

"I hope you have some better ideas," Aisha said, her voice irritated. She knocked the Hawk's head again, harder this time, so that it banged back against the tree trunk. "Benjamin is one of our own—he belongs to the Nasiris. Committing suicide isn't an option."

*Suicide.* I stared at the Hawk, my stomach churning.

His words made a thought that I'd driven to the back of my mind resurface. *What if removing myself from the equation really is the only way to solve this?*

Arron was watching me intently, clearly enjoying the effect that his words were having on me. I assumed a poker face and stared right back at him. I raised a brow and asked as calmly as I could, "Well? Is that your only suggestion?"

"That is the only foolproof suggestion that I have.

There is one other thing you could try, but there is no guarantee that it would work, or that you would even survive it. It's just a… speculation based on the vast knowledge I have of the Elders and their ways."

"What is it?" Aisha asked, glaring down at him.

"Free my limbs first." The Hawk scowled at Aisha. "Let me sit comfortably."

Aisha reluctantly lifted whatever restraint she had over him and allowed him to get to his feet. Or rather talons. *Hawks are the strangest things.* Their bodies were just like humans', and they even had normal arms and hands. But where their feet should have been were talons, and their otherwise humanoid face possessed a beak instead of a nose and mouth. And of course, they had giant wings sprouting from beneath their shoulders.

I took a step backward as I scanned Arron. He flexed his only wing, stretching it out to its full length, before walking a few feet over to a rock and sitting down. With only one wing, I wondered how he even traveled places. I guessed he must rely on others to help him get around. In any case, it meant that there was no danger of him trying to escape even after Aisha lifted her restraint.

Arron winced and breathed out slowly, as if he were in some kind of pain, before continuing. "When an Elder first imparts its nature into a victim, it's the heart where the infection settles. While I won't pretend to have come across a case quite like yours, vampire, I can say with almost complete certainty that whatever hold this Elder has over you is rooted within your heart."

Arron's words sent my mind into a tailspin. The hold that Elders had over vampires, or at least the hold my Elder had over me, felt like it transcended physicality. His influence was subtle and intangible, a part of my consciousness. It had never occurred to me to think about the physical side of how this worked, not to speak of pinpointing their influence to a specific organ. But now that Arron had told me, the heart made sense. It made total sense.

"So the heart is the center of it all," I repeated, more to help the notion sink into my own brain than for any other purpose. "It's where their influence takes root."

"Yes," Arron replied. "Hence, the primary way to kill a vampire—or a vessel, as we Hawks call them—is by piercing through its chest and destroying the heart. I'm sure you know plenty about this…" I thought back to the vampire I had just slaughtered in the Blue Tavern. My clothes were still stained with his blood. "Staking or tearing apart a vampire's heart is the most common method to rob a vampire of its immortality," the Hawk continued, "because destroying the heart also destroys the Elder's nature and influence over the vampire."

"That's why you can snap a vampire's neck and spine, or break almost any part of his body, and he will still survive," I muttered.

"That's right," Arron replied.

Aisha exhaled impatiently. "Where are you going with all this, Hawk? I already told you that suicide is not an option."

Arron slowly crossed his arm over his chest, eyeing me even as he replied to the jinni. "If you would be patient enough to listen to what I'm about to say, you will understand that I'm not suggesting suicide."

"How could a vampire live with his heart destroyed?" Julie asked, speaking up for the first time since arriving in Arron's presence.

"Obviously that's not possible… The vampire would have to live with the heart of another."

I gaped at the Hawk as his words sank in.

"What? You're talking about like a… a heart transplant?"

The words sounded crazy to me as I said them. The idea of a supernatural being undergoing a medical procedure that was common in the human world just seemed so… out of place.

"Whose heart would Ben need?" Aisha asked.

"Logically, it would need to be the heart of another vampire," Arron replied.

The heart of a vampire. My mind traveled back to the vampire I'd left paralyzed only hours ago—which was of course stupid. He had likely been found by now along with his companion's corpse as the people of The Tavern scoured the island for the culprit.

"It would also need to be a fresh heart," Arron said. "Removed not less than a few minutes before from the willing—or unwilling—donor."

My eyes narrowed on the Hawk as I wondered if I could really trust a word that he was saying. He'd made it clear that he wanted me dead. Even if we did procure the heart of another vampire, how did I know that this wasn't all a ruse? I'd had no idea that vampires could even survive such a procedure. And me lying there on some operating table with my chest cut open... I'd be utterly vulnerable. I would be relying fully on Aisha's protection.

"How can I trust you?" I asked Arron.

"I don't think you have any other choice," the Hawk said.

"So we need a vampire heart," Aisha muttered to herself more than anyone else. She had seemingly accepted Arron's words.

More than seemingly.

She spun around to face Julie, who stood behind her.

"See, Benjamin," the jinni said with a gleam in her eyes, "I told you another vampire might come in handy..."

# Chapter 17: Ben

"Aisha, no!" I yelled, leaping at the jinni as she stunned Julie's limbs and sent her falling to the ground. To my horror, Aisha manifested a knife and moved toward the vampire as though she was planning to drive it right through Julie's gut then and there.

I grabbed Aisha's arms and forced her away from Julie. Twisting her around, I glared daggers at her. "What the hell are you doing? You can't just go murdering someone like that!" *Says the man who slaughtered cells of sleeping humans a few hours ago.*

"You heard Arron," Aisha said, blood rising to her cheeks. "You need a vampire heart!"

"You're insane," I said, staring at her in exasperation. "Even leaving aside the fact that I can't allow you to murder Julie in front of my eyes, say you did successfully remove Julie's heart without damaging it, and it happened to be suitable for me, what then? Do you even have the first clue as to how you would go about this procedure?"

Aisha paused, and I could tell from the look on her face that she hadn't thought this through at all.

Perhaps Aisha's jealousy was coming into play with Julie after all. Maybe she thought that I had taken a liking to Julie, and that was why she was so quick to want to kill her.

*Stupid, impulsive girl.*

Arron chuckled behind us. "You're right, Benjamin. I doubt this jinni has knowledge of how to perform such a procedure. In fact, I wouldn't know how to do it myself. I know of only one person who might be able to help you."

Grabbing the knife from Aisha's hand and giving her one last glare, I turned back to Arron. "Who?" I asked.

"I can tell you who... But that information won't be of much use until you've considered whether or not you're willing to sacrifice another's life for your own."

I swallowed hard.

No. I couldn't do this.

"There has to be another way," I breathed. "Without sacrificing someone's life. Without murdering anyone."

Arron stood up and strode a few paces toward me. "Understand, Benjamin, that the situation you're in is grave. Very grave. A sacrifice is going to have to be made somewhere along the line—either by someone else... or you could just take the noble route and end your own life."

"If you suggest that one more time..." Aisha seethed, storming toward Arron. She levitated higher in the air and gripped him by the throat, staring him deep in the eyes. "I told you," she hissed. "Benjamin is ours." The jinni turned back to look at me defiantly. "If Arron has no other ideas, then we will just have to find a vampire to murder."

I turned away from both of them and sat down on a rock nearby. I buried my head in my hands. We'd hardly spent half an hour with Arron and this nightmare was already worsening.

How could I sacrifice another life for my own? I had already claimed more innocent lives than I could count.

I sensed Julie approach. As I looked up, she eyed me tentatively. At first I thought she had come to stand near me just to feel safe from murderous Aisha. Then she took a seat on the rock next to me.

"I don't trust this Hawk," she whispered. "I don't trust anything about him."

"Neither do I," I replied. "But as he said, I don't see what other option I have."

She chewed on her lower lip. "Even if you did undergo this weird surgery, he said there's still no guarantee that you would survive. What if something happened during the operation? You'd be totally exposed—"

"I've already considered it," I said shortly. "Until we come across a better idea, this is all we've got. Trust me," I added darkly. "I have asked around."

"Why don't we go to see a witch?" Julie pressed. "I'm sure we could find one who is willing to—"

"The doctor I speak of is a witch." Arron spoke up in reply, apparently having been listening in. "She is probably the most knowledgeable witch you'll ever come across, at least when it comes to medical matters."

"Who is she exactly?" I asked. "And where does she live? The Sanctuary?"

"Her name is Uma. She lives on her own little island, where she consults. She is known among supernaturals because she is one of the very few physicians willing to help all species. Most witches with medical knowledge refuse to help others, and will only assist their own kind. Although she is originally from The Sanctuary—a white witch, not a black witch—she moved out."

The distinction between white and black witches

was blurry for me anyway, after knowing how capable of evil both sides were.

"She lives with her sister," Arron continued. "She is neutral, not allied to any particular land or people. However, I think it's safe to say that she is not so neutral as to want the Elders to come to power again. I'm sure she will agree to help you... But as I said, first you need to decide whether or not you're willing to claim another life for yourself, because Uma doesn't take kindly to people wasting her time."

I stood up. "I just want to speak to her first," I said. "I want to ask her if there is any other way." Although I knew that it was implausible, somehow at the back of my mind I was hoping that she would have some kind of freezer stuffed with spare vampire hearts that would save us from making a kill.

"You can consult with her, of course," Arron replied. "Though I'm quite certain that you will not be able to get around murdering someone."

I turned to the jinni. Her expression was irritable, her eyes on Julie. I could see that she was tiring of this mission. She just wanted to bring me back to her home as soon as possible. She didn't understand why we couldn't just claim this perfectly good vampire heart standing right next to me.

"Have you heard of Uma?" I asked the jinni.

She shook her head. "I haven't."

"Have you?" I asked Julie.

"No," she replied, still looking highly doubtful about the whole situation.

Arron had said this witch was well known. It left me unsettled that neither of my companions had ever heard of her. It meant I was going entirely by Arron's recommendation.

"Where exactly is her island?" I asked.

"It's in the middle of nowhere," Arron said. "Extremely hard to find if you don't already know where it is… I would be willing to come with you to see her."

I didn't know whether to be thankful or suspicious over Arron's offer. My every instinct told me the latter.

# CHAPTER 18: BEN

Uma's island was strange. It was very small, and aside from a strip of sandy beaches lining its circumference, the landscape consisted of nothing but a tall hill, at the top of which was a wide, five-story grey stone castle.

After we finished taking in our new surroundings, we left the beach and began to climb up the steep slope. Arron led the way, while I walked a few steps behind him. Julie made sure that she remained at my side, away from Aisha, who hung back behind us.

"I'm starving," the jinni grumbled as we arrived at the steps leading up to the entrance of the castle.

We weren't about to go hunting for human bones, so unless she magicked some for herself she was going to have to suck it up.

Arron arrived at the wide doorstep and banged three times against the heavy oak door. We were kept waiting about two minutes before the handle clicked and the door creaked open to reveal a short, petite woman with bright red ringlets and a round, plump face. She wore a white smock with green trimming. Her light blue eyes traveled over each of us, widening as she took in Aisha.

"Do you have an appointment?" she asked.

I looked toward Arron. He shook his head. "We need to make one."

The witch opened the door wider, allowing us to step inside. We emerged in a spacious, high-ceilinged entrance room I soon realized was a waiting room. It was bare except for a wide desk at the opposite end of the room, and rows of chairs lining the walls—five of which were already occupied by what appeared to be a group of warlocks.

The witch led us over to the desk. She walked around it and sat down, pulling out a dark red ledger.

"So who is here to see my sister exactly?" she asked, donning a pair of wide-rimmed spectacles.

"Me," I replied.

"A vampire," she muttered, picking up a quill and jotting down a note on the parchment. "What is your name?"

I hesitated, wondering whether or not I ought to give my real name.

"Benjamin Novak," Arron replied for me. I threw him a sharp look, which he ignored.

"And what is your ailment?" the witch continued.

*Where do I start?*

"He requires a change of heart," Arron replied for me again.

The witch's eyebrows shot up to her frizzy hair. "Why on earth do you need that?"

Evidently, this was not a common request.

I looked around the room, not comfortable discussing these details with other strangers in the room. Before Arron could respond for me again, I replied, "I would like to speak privately with your sister about my condition."

"That's all right." She consulted her ledger again. "Well, the soonest she could see you would be the day after tomorrow."

My heart dropped. The day after tomorrow. With my predicament, that was an age away.

"I don't have that sort of time," I said, clenching my jaw. "I need to see her sooner."

"I'm afraid she won't be available," the witch replied stiffly. "The day after tomorrow, in the evening, is the soonest appointment available. You could arrive late afternoon just in case she finishes with another patient earlier... Do you want it or not?" There was a tone of impatience in her voice.

I let out a sigh. "I want it."

"Very well. I have scheduled your appointment. Now, we need to talk payment."

She reached into one of the drawers beneath her desk and pulled out a single piece of parchment. She drew three circles on it and planted it down on the counter before us. I didn't know what exactly I was expecting it to be—some kind of bill, perhaps specifying the required number of gold coins? I wasn't expecting to be staring down at some kind of bizarre ingredients list.

Most of the items scrawled on the list were completely foreign to me. I didn't have the first clue what they were. I focused on the three items that the witch had circled...

*Tooth of werewolf. One strand of merflor. Scale of dragon.*

*What the...*

Arron addressed me. "Uma asks for a rather unique way of payment. She keeps an updated list of ingredients that she requires. In return for treatment, three items from the list must be provided by each patient."

I looked down at the list again, feeling intimidated. The first was bad enough... but the scale of a dragon? And what was merflor?

"Merflor is a type of rare plant that grows in The Cove," Arron said, as though he'd read my thoughts.

"And scale of a dragon," Julie murmured.

We had dragons back in The Shade who might be willing to shed a scale for me, but going back there wasn't an option. Even if I sent Aisha, or perhaps even Julie on my behalf, it would mean explaining what was happening to me—and I just wasn't willing for my family to know how bad things had become since I'd last seen them. They would be worried enough as it was.

I continued to stare at the list disbelievingly. Those who sought out Uma were supposed to be ill. I couldn't help but wonder how she expected them to procure such fantastical items. I could only suppose that this was simply the price of her treatment. Apparently if one couldn't provide it, then it was just tough luck.

"Make sure you have them for your appointment," the witch said pointedly. "I'm afraid if you don't we will have to turn you away."

Aisha looked at the witch with deep disdain.

I had no choice but to thank the redhead and turn away.

"I'll be with you in a moment, Benjamin," Arron said.

I looked back at him. "What?"

"I need to pick up a personal health item while I'm here." He turned his focus to the witch. "Uma owes me a small favor, I'm sure you recall?"

The witch nodded. "Come with me to the apothecary," she said. Standing up, she led him through a door behind her desk. I remained in my spot, straining to hear their conversation as they walked away, but I picked up on nothing.

"We might as well wait outside," Aisha murmured, glaring at the warlocks seated in the waiting room.

We exited the building and stepped outside onto the windy hilltop. I heaved a sigh, clasping the list in my hand.

Then I turned on the jinni. "You cured River's brother of autism," I said. "Say somehow we got a suitable heart… Are you certain that you, Nuriya or anyone else in The Oasis wouldn't know how to perform this operation? Would it really be that much different than treating a human? You seem to be well-versed in human illnesses, even mental ones."

Aisha shook her head. "If you were a human, we wouldn't hesitate to use our powers. But you're not. And swapping the heart of a vampire... Well, it's kind of unheard of. Even though we could try, I don't think we would want to risk it. Nuriya wouldn't, I'm sure. Just in case we did something wrong... As much as I despise the idea of relying on a witch to do this, Ben, I think it might be the safest option."

"Assuming this witch actually has Ben's best interest in mind and doesn't deliberately jeopardize the procedure," Julie added darkly.

"Well, I will be by Ben's side observing closely," Aisha said.

Arron emerged from the castle and approached us. My eyes roamed him suspiciously, searching his hand. It was empty. He stepped forward and took the witch's list from me, glancing over it as though he hadn't left us.

I looked back at Julie. "Haven't you had enough of all this by now?" I felt uncomfortable that she was still trailing along with us. I'd hoped that she would want to back out after what Aisha had wanted to do to her—and what Aisha had made clear she still wanted to do, if I would only let her.

Julie paused, shifting her gaze from Aisha to me. There was a look of determination in her eyes, and also what I believed to be sincerity. "I'll stay," she replied. "I've come this far… I'm anxious to see how it all ends up."

*Hopefully not in a pile of rubble.*

"Tooth of werewolf," Arron interrupted. "I suggest we procure that first."

*We?*

"You're coming with us?" I asked. I had been half expecting him to ask to be returned after fixing me up with an appointment.

"Like Julie," he said, "I too am anxious to see how this ends."

There was an unsettling glint in his eyes as he glanced up at me before resuming his focus on the list.

*Tooth of werewolf.* I could hardly believe that we

were doing this. All just to get a private meeting with a witch, whom I still didn't know could help me without requiring me to murder someone. Heck, for all I knew she might not be successful in helping me even with a fresh heart. *And now these items…* "Tooth of werewolf and scale of dragon. We need to procure them without killing," I said. Even if I wanted to, I doubted we'd be able to pull off slaughtering a dragon anyway…

"The werewolf tooth and the merflor should be possible without murder," Aisha replied. "As for the dragon scale… let's just get the first two before thinking about that…"

"So we need to go to The Woodlands?" Julie asked.

"The Woodlands?" I frowned.

"That's the realm of werewolves," Julie explained.

"Yes," Arron said. "We should head there now. We might find ourselves running out of time if we dally."

On cue, Aisha made our surroundings disappear in a fog of mist, and the next thing I knew, we had arrived at the edge of a dense wood of towering trees that would rival even The Shade's redwoods. The ocean roared behind us, wild waves crashing against a pebble beach.

Arron neared and addressed me in a low voice. "You're going to need to let go of this aversion to killing," he said. "We need to get this problem solved, and since you're not open to any alternative, claiming lives—at least one life—is mandatory somewhere along the line. In fact, it would be much faster and easier to just kill a werewolf for a tooth than dancing around trying to figure out some other way."

Ignoring his words, I marched toward the entrance of the woods.

"Aisha," I called. "Come with me."

I didn't care what Arron said. During my bouts of bloodlust, one might argue that I had an excuse for murdering the way I did. But now that, thanks to Bahir, I had control over my thoughts and was aware of myself, I wasn't about to look for an excuse for killing. I simply couldn't justify it. We had to find another way.

As we entered the dense wood, I scanned the area

and began to mull over how we were going to pull off this first ingredient. The best way would be to find a werewolf who was alone and corner him or her. Aisha would need to stun the wolf and anaesthetize the jaw so the creature wouldn't feel the pain while we removed a tooth. Even that was uncomfortable to me—forcing a tooth from someone who had done no harm to me—but it was the best solution I could think of. Because I didn't think that we would find an abundance of werewolf teeth in the undergrowth. And we didn't have time to scour the place in search of one. We still had two more items to get before the appointment.

And so we moved swiftly and silently through the woods in search of our victim.

Then something occurred to me. The woods were dark due to the thick canopy of leaves overhead, but it was still daytime. If we came across a werewolf now, they would be in their humanoid form. The list stated 'tooth of werewolf.' But would the tooth be acceptable if it came from a werewolf's human form? I doubted that if I pulled a tooth while the beast was in their human form the tooth would turn into a wolf tooth once night fell. The list didn't specify, but I couldn't help but feel that the witch would want the tooth of an actual wolf… in which case we had time to kill.

"We shouldn't have come to The Woodlands first," I muttered, frustrated.

"Why?" Arron asked.

I explained to the Hawk what had just occurred to me.

"Oh," he said. "I wouldn't worry too much about that… It will take time to search out a wolf in the first place. It's already late afternoon. By the time we find a beast, the sun may have well set."

Still, I felt unsure as to whether Arron's suggestion to come here first had been wise. Julie also looked as doubtful as ever, while Aisha's eyes were narrowed in concentration as they darted around the area in search of a wolf.

***

As it turned out, Arron was right. I was both surprised and dismayed by how long it took us to track down a target. Aisha had suggested that we go straight to the mountains where the wolves' dens were, but I remained insistent on getting a wolf on his own. Approaching the dens, which would be closed off and filled with packs of dangerous wolves, was simply not a good idea. More injuries than necessary would be incurred, and if they launched a full-on attack, I was sure that at least one life would be lost.

It wasn't until the sun had set that I spotted a lone wolf through the trees, bent over and drinking from a stream. He was already in his wolf form, so we wouldn't even have to wait. I froze, holding up a hand and urging the others to stop. I was on the verge of turning to Aisha and nodding for her to stun the wolf when a twig snapped to my left. I spun around to see an apologetic Julie.

"I'm sorry," she said in a whisper.

It was too late. The werewolf's head shot up from the stream and, noticing us, he turned and raced away. I bolted after him. Although I was sure that I ran at least as fast as a werewolf, he'd had a good head start and now, as I looked around the dark tree trunks, I couldn't see him anywhere. For all I knew, he could've scampered down a secret hole somewhere. As the others appeared by my side, not even Aisha could locate the wolf.

I turned on Julie, unable to hide my irritation. "We can't afford more snapping twigs."

"I'm so sorry," she said in a hushed tone.

"Okay," I said, breathing out. "Just be careful next time."

***

We spent what felt like the next half hour continuing through the woods without coming across another wolf. I was beginning to feel desperate. I even pondered Arron's suggestion to go directly to their dens. But I didn't consider it for long.

As we entered a particularly dense area of woodland, I heard pounding in the distance. The thundering of heavy paws. I froze, raising my hands for the others to do the same. They halted and looked at me.

"Do you hear that?"

From the alarmed look on Julie's face, she too had heard it.

The noise became louder as the footsteps drew closer and closer. Soon I could make out harsh, heavy panting.

I looked up toward the treetops. "Let's climb," I whispered. I grabbed hold of the nearest branch to me and swung myself up into a tree. Julie followed closely behind me and planted herself on a nearby branch. I'd forgotten about Arron only having one arm, but Aisha helped him into a tree several feet away.

My mind worked furiously. I had to think of a plan. The lone wolf whom we'd spotted earlier—or rather who had spotted us—had likely traveled back to his pack, and now a group of them had come to investigate. And from what I could hear, it was a very large group.

This was just what I'd wanted to avoid.

The first of the pack whipped through the trees beneath us. A giant black wolf with dark green eyes ran at the forefront. They halted, apparently having picked up on our scent.

Dozens of gleaming eyes shot up toward us at once. There was no hiding from them, but at least being higher up gave us an advantage. Or at least I'd thought that it would. The black wolf—the largest and most ferocious-looking, who appeared to be the leader of the pack—launched himself at my and Julie's tree. Digging his claws into the bark, the tree trembling, he began to climb toward us.

Julie clasped my hand and tugged on it. Her hazel eyes bulging, she urged me higher up into the tree.

I extended my claws, even as I hoped that I wouldn't have to resort to violence.

The wolf was slower in climbing the tree and we gained height much faster.

"We are not here to cause trouble," I called down. "Nor are we enemies."

Arriving on one of the thick lower branches, the wolf balanced himself and paused, looking up at us.

"Then why have you come?" he growled. "Vampires aren't welcome here."

I glanced toward Aisha through the trees. She was eyeing me intently. I knew that if she suspected I was in the slightest bit of danger, she would blast the wolf out of the tree. Which was the last thing that I wanted. It would only rile them up and make our task much harder to complete.

"I simply require the tooth of a werewolf," I said. "Grant me this and we will leave in an instant."

My words only seemed to aggravate the wolf.

"What makes you think you can just arrive in our land and make demands?" he snarled. "Who do you think you are?"

*A very desperate man.*

"Maybe you could try telling them the truth," Arron called from a nearby tree, as he and Aisha retreated from two werewolves climbing up toward them.

The black wolf was already continuing his ascent toward us. It wouldn't be long now before he reached the top.

"The tooth would be put to good use," I said. "If you'll listen, I'll explain."

The werewolf didn't appear to be in any mood to listen. He was too close now—his heavy jaws within biting distance of our feet—forcing Julie and me to leap into the branches of a nearby tree. The werewolf leapt after us, landing on a wide branch several feet beneath us.

"Do you want the Elders to rise again?" I bellowed down.

The wolf froze, gazing up at me through his dark green eyes. My question had taken him by surprise.

"What kind of imbecile are you?" he hissed. "Nobody in their right mind would want that."

"Then one of you will relinquish a tooth."

He let out another deep growl and shook his fur before continuing to climb toward us.

I had to try a different tactic. Julie gasped as I leapt from our branch, and dropped down just four feet away from the wolf. Opening his jaws, he lunged forward. I dug my fingers through the thick fur on the top of his head and, using it as support, swung myself around the wolf's body and landed on his back. He twisted his head back and snapped at me with his jaws. I moved further down his long back out of reach. The wolf was forced to leap from the tree, down to the ground, where he could tackle me unimpaired by the need to maintain grip and balance on a branch.

The moment his feet touched down, I leapt off him and created a distance of ten feet between us—a distance that he immediately motioned to close.

"My name is Benjamin Novak," I said, my voice deep.

The black werewolf, along with several of his companions who'd begun to circle me, paused.

"Novak," the leader repeated. "Are you a relation of Derek Novak?"

"Yes," I said. "He is my father. I am prince of The Shade."

I'd forgotten about the visit my parents and sister had made to The Woodlands during their mission to end the black witches. According to their recounting of events, they had freed a pack of werewolves from the clutches of Rhys. I realized now that revealing that I was a Novak was the first thing that I should have done.

The beasts' mood changed drastically, and they took a step back, as though out of respect. The wolf lowered his head slightly. "Then that changes things," he said. He looked around at the rest of his companions, who had stopped chasing Aisha and Arron by now. "After what the Novaks did for one of our packs, I say we owe it to this boy to listen to what he has to say."

I maintained firm eye contact with the wolf who appeared to be the chieftain. "Thank you," I said steadily.

"I want to know why you mentioned the Elders," he said. "What exactly is the relevance of those dark spirits to your visit here?"

I steeled myself to recount my history, albeit leaving aside many of the details. I explained to them that an Elder had engulfed my heart as a newborn and created a lasting connection between us, with the intention of using me to assist them in their future resurgence.

The werewolves' eyes had darkened by the time I'd

finished. The leader's mood changed drastically. "We may be grateful to your family for the favor they did us," he said. "But we cannot ignore the evil that lives inside you, waiting to be unleashed. You say that you need a tooth in order for the witch Uma to disinfect you. But what if your plan doesn't work? I don't see a reason to not kill you right now and end this evil before it has a chance to rise…" The leader shifted his heavy paws on the soil.

Aisha swept toward me, planting herself firmly by my side. She glared daggers at the wolf.

"Just go ahead and try to kill him, wolf," she hissed. "You cannot so long as he is under the Nasiris' protection."

Perhaps the leader hadn't noticed the jinni until now, having been so focused on chasing after Julie and me in the tree. But now that he did, his stance became far less confident. His eyes darted over Aisha before he retreated a step, apparently convinced that killing me was not an option after all.

"You cannot let the Elders rise to power," he hissed at Aisha. "Why would your tribe protect him?"

"Because he has joined our family. He is one of our own," Aisha shot back. "One more mention of killing him, and you will sorely regret it."

Afraid that Aisha was about to turn murderous again, I gripped her forearm.

The werewolf backed away further.

"There is much at stake here," he said after a pause. "Much at stake…" He turned to the werewolf with brown fur standing on his right-hand side. The leader's dark face was filled with reluctance, even as he addressed his companion quietly. "We can't kill the boy with these jinn around. I don't see what other course of action we have than to grant him a tooth… and hope the doctor is competent in her task."

The brown werewolf only grunted in response, before turning and bolting away into the darkness of the woods, leaving the rest of us standing together in silence.

The leader began to pace slowly up and down in front of me. "Know that this is the first time I have ever bowed to a request from a stranger."

*That much I can believe.*

His eyes locked on mine. "Make good use of the tooth," he said, his gravelly voice intense. "Remember that far more lies in the balance than just your own life. Don't let us down."

I swallowed hard. *Don't let us down.* As I looked into his eyes, the responsibility I carried on my shoulders sank in deeper. This wolf and every other wolf surrounding me had their own lives and loved ones. Families. Children. By the mere act of keeping myself alive I was posing a danger to entire realms filled with such lives. I didn't want to think about how many could be affected if the Elder managed to lure me back to Cruor and bring his plan to fruition.

I nodded stiffly, even though I had no way of guaranteeing I could fulfill such a promise.

My situation felt completely out of my hands. It felt like I was relying on everyone but myself—Aisha, Bahir, Arron, the witch doctor... and before there had been River. After all the blood I'd consumed, I was unable to even stand on my own two feet without Bahir inside me, fighting a battle against the Elder's increasing influence over me.

This lack of control was one of the most disturbing things about the predicament that I was in. The feeling of relying on supernatural creatures I didn't even trust. Even Aisha, who was tasked to protect me, I couldn't trust fully because as loyal as she seemed to be, she possessed her own faults and weaknesses.

Everyone was depending on me, yet I couldn't depend on myself.

Yet all the while, I couldn't shake the feeling that this was a mission I was supposed to go on alone. I'd felt it deep down in my gut the night I'd told Corrine to leave The Oasis with River. I didn't know how I knew it. I just did.

But I couldn't see any way to change the situation.

The brown wolf came into view, interrupting my thoughts. As he bounded toward us through the undergrowth, he clutched a small brown sack in his mouth. He arrived in front of me and dropped it at my feet before backing away and resuming his position beside the black wolf.

I stooped down and picked up the sack from the ground. Loosening the strings, I found myself staring down at a large jagged tooth. I wasn't sure where he had gotten this from. Perhaps they had some kind of collection, or perhaps it was even from a departed wolf. I didn't care much, as long as it would satisfy the witch.

I bowed my head slightly. "Thank you," I said.

The black wolf's eyes remained boring into mine.

I wanted to feel strong in that moment, as strong as the look he was giving me. But no matter how I tried, I couldn't. How could I feel strong while being propped up by stilts?

# CHAPTER 19: BEN

I was quiet after Aisha transported us out of the woods and back to the beach. One could say that procuring this tooth had been painless, or at least more painless than I'd expected. Yet I could hardly bring myself to feel relief. My mind turned immediately to the next item we had to find for the witch.

"Merflor," I said.

"We must head to The Cove," Arron replied.

"Do you have any idea where to search for this

plant within that place?" I asked.

"I know the substance," Aisha replied before Arron could.

"I have a good idea too," Arron said.

Julie touched my shoulder. "Are you all right?" she asked, her hazel eyes traced with concern. "You look unwell."

I smiled bitterly. I'd been unwell for so long, I'd forgotten what it felt like to be well.

"I'm okay," I muttered.

"Let's get a move on then," Arron said. "We need to make sure that we have all these ingredients in time, or you will have to reschedule the appointment... and that could come with another fee."

Another fee. I didn't like the sound of that. I guessed that would involve taking off on another escapade to find some other stupid ingredient for her.

The stormy beach disappeared around me and when my vision focused again, I was standing on an islet. The slimy rocks surrounding me glistened in the moonlight. The ground swarmed with giant crabs scuttling from one shallow pool to the other. I tried to avoid stepping on any of them as I approached the edge and looked down into the water. They appeared deep and murky, filled with some kind of thick seaweed. Surrounding this islet were countless others. We were in the midst of some kind of archipelago.

"Welcome to The Cove," Aisha murmured. "The merfolk of course live in these waters. It is not advisable for anyone to enter them. So I suggest you all stay on this rock while I go down there in search of the herb."

"How long do you think this will take?" I asked.

The jinni shrugged. "I don't know. I'll be as fast as I can."

I'd heard that one before. Leaving the islet, she drifted down to the water and sank beneath it. Her long, thick hair billowed momentarily on the surface before disappearing with the rest of her.

It made sense for her to go. My parents had told me of some of the sinister creatures that lay beneath these waters, and I guessed Aisha would be immune to all of them.

I sat down on the edge of the islet and watched the waves licking the rocks. My eyes became unfocused as my mind traveled back to River. The girl I ached for. The only girl I'd ever professed my love to. I'd dated girls before River, but never come close to feeling strongly enough about them to say those three words. Although some had proclaimed love to me, I'd never been the kind of person to exaggerate feelings.

I closed my eyes, playing over in my head the last night we'd spent together. I relived her touch, her kisses, her embrace. The way she'd looked at me when she'd said she loved me too. The ache I'd felt, knowing that I had to leave her.

I snapped out of my reverie when someone sat next to me. I opened my eyes. Julie crouched, looking down into the water with a strangely thoughtful expression on her face.

"I've never seen a werewolf so cooperative," she commented.

"Have you come across many werewolves?"

"A fair number," she replied. "My father had some dealings with some. Though I've never come so close."

She paused, clasping her hands together. Then her hazel eyes raised to mine. There was an undercurrent of sympathy behind them, sympathy that made me feel deeply uncomfortable.

"Look, Benjamin," she said, catching her lower lip between her teeth. "I know you barely know me. And I know I've voiced my concern about this before. But my mother always said that my gift was my intuition, and since I'm with you on this journey, I can't hold back that I simply feel we're going in the wrong direction. This whole heart thing..." She glanced back at Arron. "I just don't see any good coming of it."

I let out a weary sigh. I'd had this conversation with her only a few hours ago.

"Julie," I said. "I know it's utterly far-fetched. Hell, I barely believe it myself. But if you had been through what I've been through, you would understand why I'm trying this."

She hesitated before continuing. "It's just that I've been thinking... I might have another idea.

Something that wouldn't involve cutting you open and messing with your heart."

"What?" I asked, sitting up straight.

"Well, it just occurred to me as we were waiting in those woods for the wolf to return with the tooth…" Her voice trailed off and she cast a glance behind her at Arron, who was standing on the other side of the islet. "I-I don't feel comfortable telling you with the Hawk listening in," she breathed.

I wondered what idea Julie could've come up with that she didn't want Arron knowing about. I didn't know how good the Hawk's hearing was, but I was quite certain he was able to hear what we were saying from this short distance.

"Julie wants to talk to me privately," I called to Arron.

I didn't wait for his response. Standing up, I caught Julie's eye and nodded toward the islet opposite us. There was a wide distance between the two, but it wouldn't take that much effort to jump it.

Arron cast Julie a suspicious glare as the two of us leapt off the islet and landed on the neighboring one about twenty feet away. Even here, I wasn't sure that we were out of earshot, and from the look on Julie's face, she wasn't confident either.

We crossed to the next islet, and then the next, until we had moved five islets away. Julie eyed Arron, standing on a rock and looking toward our direction, before she faced me.

"Well, what is it that Arron can't hear?" I asked.

She appeared tense. I wasn't sure if she was still worried that Arron might overhear us, or if it was something about what she was planning to tell me.

Her voice sounded strained as she began in a whisper, "My father was given a gift some years ago, by an old warlock who owed him a favor… It was a box, about the size of that rock over there." She pointed behind me to a large rock. "It was a beautiful box, but also sinister. The warlock said that it was crafted entirely out of human ribs and that it held a special power. A power I never believed it could possess… until I reconsidered a few hours ago when we were in The Woodlands." She paused.

"And? What power?"

She let out a breath. "I'm sure you'll find it as unbelievable as I did… But the warlock said that box was a trap specifically designed for Elders. The warlock had given it to my father soon after the demise of the Elders, once we had gotten free from our old mountain coven—or should I say prison. Knowing that we had been victims of those creatures for so long, the warlock gave it to my father as a gesture and told him that he could use it if an Elder ever found his way to us again in the supernatural world… Of course, thankfully, one never has, and so my father never put it to the test."

"A box," I repeated disbelievingly. "How could a box be capable of trapping an Elder? They aren't made of physical elements like flesh and bone. They are spirits."

"I'm not sure. Honestly, I don't know how that warlock came across the box, or how it was originally infused with such a power. He just told us what it was made of and what it was capable of doing… and he also told us how to use it."

"How?"

The vampire rubbed a palm over her forehead. "I'm just trying to recall his words..." Her face scrunched as she closed her eyes tight. "Human blood," she said after a pause. "The warlock said something about keeping the lid of the box open, and inside, placing a basin of human blood. Elders are unable to keep themselves from gravitating toward human blood, especially if fresh. If the box was in close proximity to the spirit, it would sense the blood, be drawn to it, and as soon as it entered within, the box would snap shut."

I stared at Julie. She was losing me. I hadn't thought that it was possible to top the farfetched idea of a vampire having heart surgery, but this Elder trap sure did it. The crazy things we were coming up with only highlighted the direness of my situation.

"Okay," I said, exhaling slowly. "You're not a hundred percent sure if this box really does possess the powers to trap an Elder. Your memory also seems to be hazy regarding how to work the thing... But let's just say that old warlock really did give you an Elder trap, and your memory regarding how to work it is accurate… Leaving aside the fact that we'd have to get fresh human blood, the box is still with your father, right? Do you even know where your father is?"

A look of discomfort crossed her face. "I, uh… Of course I don't know exactly where he is. I haven't seen him since I escaped but… I would imagine that he would be near The Tavern if he sent two men to come and kidnap me. His ship wouldn't have been far off that island's shore. There's no saying where he and his crew are now, but I would assume that they would still be close to that area—still looking for me." She looked down at her feet, dodging a crab as it scuttled by. "Obviously, I couldn't ask for or retrieve the box myself, but your jinni girlfriend—"

"Aisha is not my girlfriend," I corrected her.

"Sorry. Your jinni friend, I'm sure, would have no problem airlifting the box… I could tell her exactly where it's located on the ship—I don't see what reason my father would've had for moving it when it's been sitting in his study all these years."

I held up a hand, catching up with Julie's train of

thought. "Okay, so if we assumed this was a working trap, and we knew how to use it, and we managed to find the box and steal it from your father's boat without any problems, and get fresh human blood... Then what?"

"Then we would need to track down the Elder—Basilius, Arron said he was known as? He's the one who imprinted on you, and he's the one who has the influence over you. We'd need to trap him in the box."

"But even if we did manage to trap him inside it, how would that stop his influence over me? He may not be able to glide out of the box and inhabit my body, but his influence would still remain with me as it has until now."

"No." Julie shook her head. "According to what the warlock said to my father, if an Elder was trapped inside this box, it would be truly trapped. Contained. It would not be able to have any influence on the world outside the box. That's what was supposed to be so special about the gift."

I couldn't shake my skepticism, in spite of how

sincere Julie appeared. "Let's say everything you've told me so far is correct, how would we actually get an Elder to enter the box? We are nowhere near Cruor."

My voice trailed off at the somber look on Julie's face.

"We would use you as bait," she said, "but we would have to travel to Cruor in order to get close enough to do this."

At this, I shook my head. "No. Julie, I appreciate you trying to help me with this, but I can't possibly risk setting foot in Cruor."

According to the visions imparted to me by the jinn and my visit to the oracle, Basilius was currently the only Elder in Cruor who was strong enough to inhabit a vessel. So while I wouldn't be in danger from other Elders there, the moment Basilius sensed my closeness, even the jinn wouldn't be able to stop him from entering me fully and finally claiming me the way the oracle had prophesied.

"I know it's not the simplest of solutions," Julie said. I almost laughed. "But as crazy as it sounds, I thought it might be less risky than having your chest sliced open by a stranger who could be allied with a Hawk who clearly wants you dead."

"I was willing to consider the box idea until you mentioned Cruor. As dangerous and uncertain as removing my imprinted heart would be, it still feels like the less risky option."

Julie shrugged. "Fair enough. I thought I ought to mention it to you all the same."

Having made up my mind, I looked toward the islet where Arron was waiting. He had begun pacing up and down over the rocks. "You didn't want Arron overhearing this because…?"

"Because I don't want him knowing about this box," Julie replied. "As much as I dislike my father, he is after all my father. I wouldn't want to be responsible for setting a gang of Hawks on him."

That was understandable.

"So… that was everything you wanted to say to me?" I asked, my eyes traveling back to Julie's pale face.

Clenching her jaw, she nodded.

I was unsure of what to say next. I'd already thanked Julie for her concern and it felt awkward to be standing alone with her in silence. I would prefer for there to be a third person present as we waited— even if that person was Arron. I gestured to the islet and the two of us leapt back toward it.

Now we could only wait for Aisha to return.

# CHAPTER 20: BEN

As I had feared, we were waiting hours for the jinni. I ended up passing the time sitting opposite Julie on the rocks, with her telling me more about her life before she'd become a vampire, while Arron continued to brood behind us. Like so many, Julie's life had been ordinary before she'd become a bloodsucker at seventeen. She had been born in central China; her father had been a politician, her mother a schoolteacher. She'd gone to school and studied hard to please her parents, all while fostering the dream of becoming a ballet dancer. It was during a vacation near the Taihang Mountains, while enjoying an evening walk with her family, that her uneventful life had been turned upside down.

I found her history interesting, yet as she talked, I felt distant. My mind constantly returned from her story to my present nightmare.

By the time Aisha returned, the sky was brightening. The jinni manifested herself a few feet away from Julie and me, holding a thin violet weed.

"What took you so long?" I asked, eyeing the odd plant.

Dripping wet, Aisha approached me with a grumpy expression. She pulled away the brown sack containing the werewolf tooth that I had attached to my belt. Opening the sack, she slipped in the merflor before handing it back to me.

"Merfolk don't exactly welcome trespassers asking for directions to their valuable resources," she said, a scowl on her face. "I'm not familiar with these waters and it took a while to find."

I should have just been relieved that she had found

it. We didn't have a lot of time left. My appointment with the witch doctor was already tomorrow.

I turned to Arron, who had been quiet ever since Julie and I had left him alone to talk. I found myself wondering whether he had overheard our whispered conversation.

"So now we are on to the dragon scale," I said, trepidation filling my stomach. "Where do you suggest we get that from? Would we need to go to The Hearthlands?"

"I don't think that's a good idea," Arron replied, clearing his throat.

"Then?"

I looked toward Aisha, wondering if she had any ideas. She looked blankly back at me. "My tribe hasn't had dealings with dragons," she said. "I don't know a lot about the creatures. I'm not sure where we would find a dragon other than The Hearthlands."

"I know one we could visit," Arron said. All eyes turned on him as he continued. "His name is Breccan. He lives alone on a small, deserted island. He was banished from The Hearthlands many years ago for treason. He is an old beast, though still ferocious. However, we stand the best chance of getting what we're after from an island populated by just one fire-breather than an entire country filled with them."

"And do you know how to get to this island?" I asked the Hawk.

To my relief, he nodded. I'd never thought that I would feel grateful for a Hawk's presence—least of all Arron's—but this man was turning out to be invaluable to us on this crazy journey.

# Chapter 21: Ben

Arriving on top of a cliff, we had a full view over Breccan's mountainous island and the miles of ocean that surrounded it. We were silent as we took in the atmosphere. It was larger than I had expected. I wondered where exactly the dragon resided.

Arron clutched my shoulder as I moved to begin climbing down the rocks. "Wait," he whispered. "Let's agree on a plan."

"Do you know where Breccan is?" I asked, hoping that we could procure the witch's last request with the least amount of violence.

"That's what we need to find out," Arron replied. "He lives somewhere within the mountains. We need to scope out this place and find an entrance." His eyes traveled to the steep slope. "Though if we're lucky, we might even find a scale Breccan has already shed on the ground somewhere…. Let's start looking around this peak. And keep a sharp ear out. The shifter might not be in his beastly form—which would make him quieter and harder to detect from a distance."

With that, Arron walked forward, gesturing for us to follow. We made our way down the mountain, casting our eyes about for shed dragon scales or any sign of an entrance.

We searched for hours, long after the sun rose in the sky. Aisha cast shade over Julie and me, although the heat was unbearable. It seemed to be emanating not only from above, but also from beneath us. I wondered what kind of furnace there must have been within the mountain. After the sun reached its peak in the sky and sank low again, we still hadn't found a scale, although Arron had spotted a tunnel entrance—about the shape and size of a normal doorway.

What we had to do next became clear. We couldn't waste any more time hoping to come across a scale outside—we had to enter the caves and try to find one within. I hoped that there would be more lying around in there, and we wouldn't actually have to come face to face with the creature. The four of us gathered together on a ledge just beneath the entrance.

"We can't enter it now," Arron whispered. "We should wait for when the dragon is most likely to be asleep."

Wait. I never thought that I could despise a word so much.

"And when is the dragon likely to be asleep?" I asked tensely.

"In the early hours of the morning." Arron looked sideways along the mountain slope. "I suggest that we set up camp nearby for the night... It's evening now anyway. Before we know it, it'll be time to return."

It certainly wasn't wise to set up too close to the entrance, so Aisha transported us about a mile away. We found another ledge of a neighboring mountain that was almost opposite to the tunnel entrance. The first thing I did was make sure Aisha concealed the enclosure with her powers so no onlooker could see us resting here.

Julie pushed back her bangs with the back of her hand, wiping beads of sweat away from her forehead. She let out a weary sigh and slumped down against the wall. Arron also took a seat, stretching out his legs. Aisha said she wanted to look around the area longer, assuring me that she'd return immediately if I touched my gold band.

I didn't know what to do. I didn't feel like sitting or standing. Heck, I didn't feel like *being*.

I ended up pacing up and down the wide ledge until the sky darkened and the moon rose. Arron started a fire, after which Aisha soon returned.

She looked more irritable than ever. "I'm hungry," she said, her voice bordering on whining.

I wasn't sure what to suggest. With those jaws, I'd

imagine that she could eat anything. "You should go eat some leaves, or bark or… rocks."

"Jinn don't eat those things," she snapped, crumpling on the ground.

"I'd offer you some of my blood, but—"

She threw me a look of disgust before I could finish my sentence. "Not even your blood could tempt me, dear," she said. "I'd rather eat rocks than drink vampire blood."

"Then why not just magick yourself some bones? Fulfill your own wish."

"I want my sister to cook for me," she moaned.

*What a fusspot.*

I shrugged and sat down close to the edge of the platform, my feet hanging down. Julie was curled up in one corner, resting her head against a stone. Although her eyes were closed, I doubted that she was sleeping. I wondered when she'd last had blood.

If Arron was hungry, he didn't show it. He just sat in front of the fire, staring into the flames.

I turned my back on everyone and looked out toward the mountain opposite us.

Aisha continued grumbling to herself for the next hour before she slid up against a corner and closed her eyes. That left just me and the Hawk awake. I had been avoiding looking at him, but to my dismay, he stood up and approached me. He sat down three feet away, joining me in watching the tunnel opening.

I shifted a few inches from him, feeling unsettled by his presence. He cleared his throat.

"There's probably a fifty percent chance that you would survive the surgery if the witch agrees to do it," he said in a low voice.

*Thanks for that piece of information.* As if my mind wasn't already weighed down enough. I gritted my teeth and shot him a glare. "And your point is?"

He shrugged. "No point in particular…" His hand traveled into the folds of his robe, and when it reappeared, he was clasping a small glass bottle filled with a light blue, transparent liquid. I stared at it, wondering if it was some kind of alcoholic beverage he'd carried with him from Aviary. But he made no motion to break open the lid and take a swig. He just held it in his hand, cradling it in his palm and swishing the liquid as he stared down at it.

"Fate doesn't have to be as straightforward as life or death," he said slowly.

I furrowed my brows.

"Sometimes there can be… other choices," he continued. His eyes took on a glaze, his expression calm and relaxed, as he continued rolling the liquid. "Like humans, supernaturals can sometimes contract dangerous and fatal diseases. Diseases that make life unworthy of living. That make one wish he could give up his body entirely just to no longer feel the pain… But death is a scary thing." He glanced at me casually, though his grey eyes gleamed. "Nobody knows what truly lies beyond death. So, understandably, it's the nature of living beings to want to cling to what they know, however miserable an existence they might be leading."

I still wasn't sure where he was going with this, though I understood why he was talking in such a hushed tone. He didn't want Aisha to overhear what he was saying.

He held the potion higher and looked at it thoughtfully. He let out a slow, deep breath. "This potion," he said, "I considered taking it a number of times after the war with the Elders, and after I lost half of myself…" His expression filled with bitterness as he eyed the stump where his arm had been, and gestured his head backward to his missing wing. "The physical pain was only half of the agony. It was the mental pain that crushed me. The feeling of defeat, it was enough to destroy anyone's soul." He twisted to face me fully and caught my gaze again, his sharp eyes filled with intent. "Do you know what this is, Benjamin?" he asked, more quietly than ever.

"Why would I know?" I looked back at him warily.

"Would you like to know?"

"What is it?" I asked, taking the bait.

"It's a remedy administered by witch doctors. I picked up this bottle from Uma's sister while we were on her island. It's intended for those who no longer wish to live, but are too afraid to die. It allows for a kind of existence between the two states, in that elusive place between life and death. Where there is peace, lightness, absence of pain…"

Slowly I caught on to his train of thought. "You mean, like… a ghost?"

He looked pleased by my question. He nodded. "Like a ghost. This remedy detaches a person's soul from their body and allows him to continue living in a subtle state, without a physical, tangible form, and hence also without pain." He must have noticed the dazed expression on my face. "Understand, Benjamin, that there is much more to all of us than flesh and blood. There is the mind, the consciousness, the soul. Do you really think that when this body expires, *you* cease to exist? That you fall into some oblivion, as if you had never been alive at all? No. There is a place beyond death for all of us, whether we be humans, or supernaturals… But as I said, most aren't willing to find out."

He paused, and as he did I realized just how engrossed I had been in his words, in spite of how strange they were. I found myself impatient for him to continue.

He nodded back down to the potion. "Those who

take this elixir wish to stay in their former lives, but without the burden that comes with the physical body."

My mouth felt dry as he picked up the vial and placed it on the ground, close to me. He stood up. Again his movement was casual as he glanced down at me, though his eyes were anything but. "Just something to think about," he said, before turning and heading back to the fire, where he resumed his seat in front of it.

I stared down at the small glass bottle. The firelight danced in the innocent-looking light blue liquid.

My mind was still reeling from what Arron had told me. *Ghosts? And this potion…* That was what he'd seen Uma's sister for. A potion created by the witch. It appeared as though, if there was any truth in Arron's words, supernaturals used this potion as a kind of mercy killing… except it wasn't exactly killing. The person was supposed to live on as a ghost.

My fragmented mind, already blown to pieces by

revelation after revelation over the past few days, had just splintered further. I didn't know how much more my brain could handle before it exploded.

*So ghosts really do exist?* But, according to Arron, not everybody became a ghost. When a human or supernatural died a normal death, they left for... the beyond, wherever Arron thought that was. Becoming a ghost wasn't a natural consequence of dying. It had to be forced... by this potion? *Could this really be true?*

If taking it separated a person from their body, if I took it and became a ghost, my vampire form would become a corpse I guessed. Elders couldn't inhabit the corpses of vampires. Corpses were useless to them. That much I knew from what my parents had told me of the creatures, and all that I'd learned so far from the oracle and the jinn. Elders needed both body and soul together in order to take over. That was why they abandoned vessels when they became too weak from habitation and the vampire expired.

Despite myself, I reached toward the potion and held it in my palms.

*Could this small bottle of liquid really contain that sort of power?*

I wondered what taking it would feel like. *Would there be pain? Would it be like dying except you remained conscious? Can other people see ghosts? Can ghosts even see, talk, or feel in any way?*

I shuddered, disturbed that I'd fallen into thinking in such depth about Arron's words. I swallowed hard, a part of me tempted to plant the bottle right back down on the ground where Arron had left it.

But another part of me, the more desperate part, gripped the small bottle more tightly and stowed it in the pocket of my robe.

# CHAPTER 22: BEN

I tried to turn my mind to other thoughts than the conversation I'd had with Arron. I reached for the brown sack fastened to my waist and opened it up, gazing down at the two ingredients we had managed to gather so far. I reached inside and wrapped my fingers around the merflor. I'd expected it to be slimy, but now that it was dry, it was soft, almost velvety.

"Hey." Julie's soft voice came from behind me. "Are you okay?" She approached and took a seat on the ledge by my side.

Okay? I wasn't sure that I would ever be okay.

"Yes," I muttered.

I continued examining the merflor before moving on to the tooth, not paying much attention to Julie. I didn't want companionship. I just wanted to be on my own. If it had been possible, I would be around no one right now. I'd be on this journey alone, as I'd sensed that I ought to be right from the start.

Julie wasn't intrusive, however. She kept her distance and looked away from me, fixing her eyes on the rocky landscapes surrounding us.

I was surprised that it was me who ended up breaking the silence.

"Don't you have any plans for your life?" I asked.

She looked my way before releasing a sigh. "I'm not sure what plans I could have," she replied, her voice subdued. "I've lived the last decades of my life—ever since I became a vampire—in the shadow of my father. I've hardly been in an environment conducive for making dreams… or friends for that matter. You've probably noticed that I'm socially awkward."

Julie was shy and hesitant at times, though I wouldn't have described her as socially awkward. She'd struck up a conversation with me back in the pub in The Tavern, and then extended her help to me—a total stranger. Not exactly what an introvert would do.

"I hadn't noticed," I muttered.

A small smile curved her lips. "Good. Because I'm trying to leave behind the old me. The me who lived at the mercy of my father, bending over backward to satisfy his every demand... When I was younger—at least, when I was still a human, before we all got turned—he was strict and concerned that I always studied hard at school, like any good Chinese parent, but he was nowhere near the control freak he is now. Something just... switched in him after he became a vampire. I guess sometimes the newfound strength goes to people's heads. They become monsters—not just on the outside, but on the inside too." She paused, glancing at me. "Sorry, I'm rambling. I don't mean to bore you with more about me."

Truth be told, I was starting to feel grateful for her interrupting my silence. Her talking helped to distract me from the conversation I'd had with Arron, which was still playing in the back of my mind.

"That's all right," I told her honestly. "You're not boring me... I have to say that in spite of your sheltered upbringing, you have uncommon courage to follow me on this journey."

She smirked. "Or uncommon desperation. I do mean it when I say I have nowhere else to go. But, somehow, I came across you and we wound up getting stuck together... I don't know. Call it fate, guts, or desperation... This just feels like the right path for me to take at present."

She pulled her dangling legs up from over the edge of the ridge and twisted to face me. Her expression became serious. "I overheard what Arron said to you," she said, dropping her voice to a whisper. "I hope that you wouldn't consider doing it." She leaned in closer to me, her eyes wide with concern.

I didn't answer.

"I don't know you well, Benjamin. But I don't

need to in order to feel that you're a good person," she pressed. "I would to hate to see you go down that path… You deserve so much more."

She placed her right hand over mine where it rested on the ground. I flinched, withdrawing my hand. I felt uncomfortable with her sudden proximity, almost claustrophobic, despite sitting out in the open. I averted my gaze and stood up, turning my back on her. I walked away, past the fire where Arron sat, and moved as far away from everyone as I could on this mountain ledge. I stared down at the steep drop near my feet.

My fists clenched, my hand tightening around the brown sack of ingredients that was still in my hand.

*The surgery has to work. It just has to…*

I almost lost my footing as a stabbing pain surged in my stomach. It was excruciating, as though someone was twisting a knife into my gut. I staggered back, dropping the brown sack. I let out a low groan, falling to my knees and doubling over.

"Benjamin!" Julie's voice came from behind me, followed by Aisha and Arron hurrying over. I rolled over, lying on my back and clutching my chest, gasping for breath. I shut my eyes tight, as though that would help to contain the pain.

"Bahir!" Aisha gasped.

My eyes shot open to see Bahir emerging from my chest and hovering in front of me. His strong body was limp, practically sagging, as he floated next to Aisha. His dark hair was as messy as a bird's nest, and his previously vibrant face appeared ragged and worn. His chest and back heaved as he panted.

"I had to take a break," he wheezed, looking from me to Aisha. "I am—"

My brain didn't register any other words. A black film came down over my vision, the agony in my stomach spreading to my chest and shooting pain through my entire body. I found myself shooting to my feet even in spite of the ache, and the next thing I knew, I'd leapt from the ledge. I dove in a free fall, whizzing past the mountainside, until I landed with as much ease as a cat on a boulder at the foot of the cliff we'd been perched on. I didn't pause for a second or glance back up at the distance I'd just jumped. All I knew was that I had to escape. I had to get off of this island. I had to…

Visions of a barren land of sharp-peaked black mountains and a red-tinged sky blasted through my mind.

*Cruor.*

*I need to get to Cruor.*

I dashed forward over the rocky terrain with lightning speed. My legs assumed a mind of their own. Everything around me was a blur, the wind almost painful as I sliced through it.

Then something hit me hard on the back of my head and threw me off balance. I took a misstep and slipped on a rock. I stumbled, falling to the ground. My limbs, as if electrified, barely registered the fall. I sprang back up instantly and moved to continue hurtling forward.

But I couldn't. Aisha appeared directly in front of me, holding out both hands. My limbs had frozen, and I couldn't budge an inch. I tried to shout, yell curses at the insolent jinni for impeding my way, order her to let me pass, but I couldn't even move my mouth.

And then she ran at me. Her body became translucent at the last second, and she dove into my chest, her body melding with mine as she vanished inside of me. A growl escaped my lips, but as the last of her blue mist soaked into my chest, the pain tearing me up subsided.

It happened so suddenly it came as a shock. My vision focused again and I looked around me at the unfamiliar setting. I could barely even remember how I'd gotten down here.

*What just happened to me? Why did Bahir exit me? And now Aisha is inside me?*

I caught sight of Bahir and Julie hurrying toward me among the rocks. Bahir reached me first and gripped my arm. Despite his appearance, his grasp still had surprising strength.

"Come with me," he said.

"What just happened?" I panted.

"Let's get back to our base first." His light mist surrounded me and a moment later, he'd transported the three of us back to the ledge, where Arron was standing tensely by the fire.

"What was that?" I repeated.

"I'm sure that Nuriya explained to you that I could only inhabit you and fight off the Elder for so long," Bahir said. "I was losing all strength. I had to leave you. Aisha has taken my place inside you to continue fighting the battle for me until I have regained enough strength to resume the task."

"That pain," I breathed. "It was more consuming than I'd ever felt before. And—"

"Because the Elder is more desperate for blood than ever before," Bahir said. "He knows he is on the edge of success. You are in the supernatural realm now, closer to Cruor than ever before. He sees this as merely the last stretch before you return to him. He is calling you back, Benjamin, now more than ever."

Bahir's words sent chills running down my spine.

Even as I was still registering what had just happened, I glanced down at my chest. *Aisha... that girl is inside me now.* That was a bizarre enough notion to wrap my mind around in and of itself.

My legs still felt unsteady. Snatching up the brown

sack of ingredients I'd dropped to the ground, I re-fastened it to my belt securely and sat down. I was grateful that my three companions gave me space, though I sensed Julie's anxious gaze roaming me.

Bahir's relinquishing his hold on me had come when I'd least expected it. I had been aware that he couldn't keep up the fight forever… I supposed I had just lulled myself into a false sense of security. His leaving me on my own, completely at the mercy of the Elder's influence, had given me another harrowing taste of what my life would be like if I ever got separated from these jinn. It served as a terrifying reminder of how dependent I'd become, and how close I was to the precipice with every breath I took.

# Chapter 23: Ben

Bahir hadn't been able to follow what had happened since we'd left The Oasis. He said that the strain of remaining inside me and stifling the Elder's influence hadn't left him with the energy to pay attention to what was going on outside. He had many questions, so I gave him a brief overview of everything that had transpired since he merged into me back in the desert. After I'd finished my explanation, the next few hours passed in silence until the early morning hours arrived and Arron indicated that we should head to the entrance of the tunnel.

I was so used to having Aisha by my side, out of instinct I found myself looking around the ledge for her, only to remember that Bahir would assist me now. He transported us away from our camp and made us appear right outside the dark entrance of the tunnel. My pulse quickened as I gazed into its shadowed depths.

"Are you certain there is only one dragon living here?" I asked Arron in a whisper.

"I am not sure of anything," Arron replied curtly. "But based on the rumors I've heard, Breccan lives here by himself."

I entered the crevice first, walking slowly along the gravelly ground and trying not to crunch too much. The tunnel was narrow, forcing us to walk in single file. I wondered whether there was any entrance in these mountains big enough for the shifter to squeeze into as a dragon. If not, Breccan must've changed back into his humanoid state when entering and exiting his home.

We reached a fork in the path. I glanced at Arron

for his opinion. He nodded to our right. Since I had no idea, we went with the Hawk's suggestion. This tunnel was longer, more winding, and sloped gradually downwards. As we descended, the heat that emanated from the walls, ceilings and floors of the tunnel intensified.

I kept my ears peeled for any sound of life. All the while, we looked out for any scales that could be lining the ground, although it was highly unlikely that we would find any in this tunnel. It was far too narrow for the shifter to fit in whilst in his dragon form. Still, it didn't stop our eyes from roaming.

As we descended deeper, I began to hear what I was both hoping for and dreading. A deep, rumbling noise that vibrated the ground beneath our feet.

At least we were heading in the right direction.

As we turned a particularly sharp corner, we met a heavy iron door. My skin broke out into a sweat, something that rarely happened to me as a vampire. As I reached out a hand and brushed it against the iron entrance, it felt like the door to an oven.

Still, we had no choice but to enter. I looked

toward Bahir and whispered, "We can't risk opening the door." First of all, it might be locked, but secondly and more importantly, I was sure that it would make a horrible creak that would echo right through the mountain.

Bahir nodded, and it unnerved me how unsettled he looked. He, a jinni.

His veil of smoke fell around us and before I even had time to prepare myself for what might be on the other side, my feet planted on the ground again. A dense fog of dry heat engulfed us. It was like being in a sauna with the heater blasting at three times its maximum temperature. My throat felt so raw, I was practically panting like a dog. I had to blink constantly just to keep my eyeballs from drying out.

We had entered a massive cavernous chamber with a circular border and high rocky ceilings. Along its border was a wide raised platform lined with beacons of fire. Below were wide stone steps leading down to the center where, curled up on a heaping pile of furs, lay a sleeping dragon. Fearsomely beautiful, his scales were a brilliant magenta peppered with speckles of bright yellow. Even while sleeping, the beast exuded an impossible heat.

I forced my eyes away from the stunning creature to look more carefully around the vast cave.

*A scale.*

*We need a scale.*

I was desperately hoping that we would find one on the ground in what was apparently his bedroom—where he moved and slept in his dragon form. If we didn't find one here, I didn't know where we would. And if we couldn't find a scale that he'd already shed, we'd have only one option left. Something told me that this dragon would not be as amenable as the wolves to relinquishing a piece of his body... It wasn't like I could use the Novak card this time either. Our island was allied with dragons, but they were dragons of The Hearthlands. If anything, mentioning Breccan's compatriots could just make the situation worse after he'd been exiled by them.

I looked toward my companions, who were also scoping out the room. We split in two directions; Bahir and Arron went right, Julie and I went left. We all moved as noiselessly as possible, keeping to the raised platform that lined the edge of the cave—as far away as we could from the dragon. Julie and I searched in every shadowy corner we came across, every tucked-away crevice, every inch of the ground, but by the time we met up with Bahir and Arron again, we'd found not one single scale. Neither had they.

I turned my focus back on the center of the cave. Previously I'd been so occupied with staring at the dragon, I hadn't noticed a pile of armor near his bed—armor that would only fit him in his human form, being clearly made for a man. Gem-studded helmets, silver chest plates, golden sheathed swords and wide, diamond-encrusted shields were just some of the objects I recognized. Then, also near his bed, there was a wide pit filled with gleaming jewels. Perhaps these were possessions he'd taken with him when he'd left The Hearthlands. The only possessions... Other than the cluster of armor and the jewels, the chamber was quite empty.

My heart catapulted into my throat as the dragon's

spear-like tail moved. It extended past the furs and outward to graze the stone floor.

I feared for a moment that we had made too much noise and had woken Breccan. But then the tail settled, the dragon's breathing returning to its previous slow rhythm.

Bahir gripped my shoulder. Leaning closer, he breathed, "Arron and I will search the border once more for a shed scale, just in case we missed something."

They left Julie and me alone. My mind worked furiously as I tried to think what our next move should be.

"What now?" Julie mouthed, the beacons' firelight dancing in her hazel irises.

My throat tightened as I glanced back at the dragon. I was beginning to believe that we would have no choice but to attempt to pluck a scale directly from his body, when I caught sight of something on the bed of furs, just beneath his right hind leg.

I thought my eyes might be tricking me as I took a step closer. No. There it was. A small pile of dry scales, discolored compared to the rest of his skin. I couldn't see them before because his tail had been covering them. It was as if he was hoarding them for some reason. From where I stood, each of the scales looked bigger than my hand, but we only needed one of them. And now that Breccan had shifted…

I moved forward, gesturing for Julie to stay where she was. I descended the steps toward the dragon's bed, all the while keeping a close eye on the beast's lethal tail, which, at least for now, seemed to be remaining dormant. I paused when I reached the beginning of the fur spread. I'd miscalculated the distance from the pile of scales to the ground. The many layers of the thick fur propped the dragon up so high that, as tall as I was, I wouldn't be able to reach the scales without actually stepping onto his bed. I didn't dare to do that in case he sensed the movement.

*I should leave this task to Bahir.* He could float noiselessly and pick up one of the scales. I turned my back on the dragon so I could scan the borders of the cave. Bahir and Arron were just finishing their second circuit around the chamber. I caught the jinni's eye and beckoned him over.

"Watch out!" Julie hissed to my left.

I spun around, expecting the dragon's tail to have shifted again. Instead, as I twisted it was to face a snake. A monstrous cobra, its scales green as ivy. Its head reared and long fangs bared, it towered above me. The creature must have been twenty feet long.

Everything that happened next was a blur. I lunged for the snake, attempting to slice off its head before it caused a commotion and woke the dragon, but it was too late. Julie's warning had already done that.

The dragon let out a deep grumble. Throwing caution to the wind, I leapt for the pile of scales and grabbed one, tucking it into my belt before turning round to fight off the snake. As it sprang toward me, I latched onto its head with my claws. Now I became so preoccupied trying to stop the cobra from biting off my face as it engulfed me in its coils that I wasn't able to raise my head to see what the dragon did next or why Bahir hadn't immediately come to assist me. But as the temperature in the room spiked, I soon realized.

Bright flames engulfed the atmosphere. Breccan bellowed. Desperately, I fought with the snake as it continued to wrap itself even more tightly around me. I didn't know exactly where the dragon was— only feet away by the sound of it—and now flames impaired my vision. All I knew was that I had to get out of his path. This snake's skin was tougher to claw through than I'd expected and I couldn't afford to stay where I was.

I forced the snake and me to roll across the floor toward the pit of gems. The ground disappeared as I tipped us over the edge. We fell sideways onto the lumpy bed. More flames erupted overhead as the snake's jaws extended wide. Grunting, I managed to position my claws beneath the snake's soft throat and dug into it. The reptile's hold on me loosened and it began writhing as blood spilled from its throat, spraying my face and clothes.

I heaved its thick body off me, leaving it to die as I sat up. All I saw surrounding the outside of the pit was a solid wall of flames. I had no idea what had happened to the others. But wherever they were, the whole room appeared to be ablaze. I coughed and choked. The lack of oxygen was beginning to suffocate me in this low pit.

I couldn't see where the dragon was through the flames, but I could hear him continuing to roar and release more fire. I reached for my gold band and brushed my thumb against the snake's head.

"Come on, Bahir. Come on," I breathed.

Where was he? He should have rushed to me the moment he saw the snake attack me. Could he have gotten caught up in the flames?

The dancing wall of fire encroached further around the pit. Soon flames had reached the edge and began to lick the sides of the walls, scorching my face and stealing my breath. My skin felt like it was starting to melt.

Aisha couldn't help me even though she was inside me. She was too preoccupied with the Elder to be aware of what was going on outside. That much I already knew.

I was going to have to jump into the wall of flames

and hope the fire didn't reach my heart before I arrived at the exit. I couldn't afford to wait any longer for Bahir.

It felt like suicide, but if I stayed here any longer, the flames would take my life anyway. It was better to go out while trying to escape.

Steadying my feet, I was about to plunge into the fire when a figure clad in armor leapt through the burning wall and clattered down on the gems a few feet away. When the helmet was removed, I realized that it was Julie. Her hair was soaked with sweat, her face singed as she thrust a wide, heavy shield into my hands.

"Come," she said breathlessly. "We must hurry!"

I held up the shield in front of me as Julie grabbed my hand and we leapt headfirst into the inferno.

# Chapter 24: Ben

Even with the armor and our supernatural speed, I thought we would be consumed. The entire room was flooded with flames, and the dragon was still rampaging what sounded like only feet away from us, filling the chamber with yet more heat—apparently the temperature hadn't quite climbed high enough for him.

I kept the shield firmly in front of me. Since I didn't have a helmet as Julie did, she was my eyes. She led me forward, darting between the pockets in the room that hadn't yet been completely scorched. I still had no way of knowing what had happened to Bahir or Arron as Julie and I reached the iron door. I breathed out in relief, only to realize that it was locked.

A deafening roar sounded, followed by a gust of hot wind. The dragon's breath. I looked up to see him standing ten feet away, visible through the haze of flames and smoke, his yellow eyes gleaming with fury.

His tail lunged toward us. Julie and I flung ourselves in opposite directions, narrowly avoiding being pierced. The dragon was going to stake us before burning our corpses to ashes.

"Duck!" I yelled to Julie as the tail swished toward us again. It clinked against my shield with such force, the shield went flying out of my hand.

"Why are you here? And whose blood stains your skin?" Breccan boomed down at me. His hand shot out, motioning to grab me by the waist. I dodged him, only to find myself stuck in a corner. His plan, I was sure.

"Tell me," he continued. "Did you murder Lambas?"

*Lambas?* Despite my panic, I was momentarily taken aback by the question.

"Answer me!" he roared, scorching my eyeballs with his breath.

*Maybe that cobra was Lambas. I just murdered his pet.*

His jaws opened, revealing layers of razor sharp teeth.

"You killed her!" he repeated, his voice dripping with rage. "Didn't you?"

A pointed object flew from my left toward the dragon and struck him in the eye. Breccan bellowed in pain and staggered back. I looked up to see Bahir hovering overhead. I was shocked by his bedraggled appearance. His skin was singed almost black. Of all of us, I hadn't expected him to get injured by the flames. I could only think that he'd gotten caught by some before he'd managed to vanish himself.

*Thank God.*

Distracted by the pain, the dragon staggered

backward, his tail flailing and narrowly missing my gut. I ducked down low on the ground as Bahir approached me. Julie hurried over—accompanied by Arron, who, like Julie, had somehow managed to reach the armor. I wasn't sure how the Hawk managed to put it all on with one arm, but he wore a helmet and chest plate, as well as plates on his legs and knees.

Before the dragon could cause us any more damage, we gathered together and Bahir vanished us from the burning chamber.

# CHAPTER 25: BEN

We reappeared back at our camp. I dropped to my knees, breathing out in relief as I felt the brown sack and the dragon scale still fastened securely to my belt. I placed both on the ground and rolled over on my back, breathing in the fresh air.

*If a patient didn't require this doctor's help before an appointment, he sure as hell would need it after.*

I removed my singed cloak and peeled off my shirt, using the latter to wipe down my face, which felt burnt to a crisp. I had a nasty burn that stretched from the base of my neck down to the middle of my chest, as well as on my hands and arms.

Julie had been covered with armor, but even still her face and hands were badly burnt. Out of all of us, Arron seemed to have gotten off lightest. Bahir healed his own skin before moving to me. He brushed his hands along my burns—causing them to sting horribly—before the burns disappeared. I was glad I didn't have to wait for my body's own healing capabilities to kick in. It would only exacerbate my craving for blood—which was already starting to come on full force again after the exertion I'd just put my body through.

After Bahir had finished with Arron, Arron approached and looked down at the scale. He bent down and picked it up, examining it in his hand.

"I'll take care of this for now, shall I?" the Hawk offered. "It's too big to fit in that sack and it shouldn't be bent."

I shook my head. "No, I'll keep it with me." After all the trouble we'd gone through to get it, I didn't want to let it out of my sight.

Raising a brow, Arron placed it back down on the ground next to the brown sack.

Once I'd rested my limbs a little and regained my breath, I sat up.

"Are you okay?" Julie asked, leaning against the cliffside wall a few feet away.

I nodded. "Thank you," I said, "for helping me back there."

"That's okay."

Picking up the sack and fastening it back to my belt, I tucked the scale beneath my arm and stood up. I walked to the border of the ledge and gazed out at the brightening sky. I was surprised that the dragon hadn't come out of the cave to look for us.

"So today is the day you have an appointment with the witch doctor, correct?" Bahir asked, moving next to me.

"Yes, today." The time had flown by, and in the end it was a good thing that the doctor hadn't been available before now. We would not have been ready.

"I suggest that we rest here a little longer," Arron said, taking a seat and stretching out his legs. "We still have hours to pass before the appointment."

Although I was raring to go, we could all do with more rest. I for one could hardly remember the last time I'd slept properly and although I wouldn't be able to sleep, at least I could rest my eyes. I walked over to my cloak and wrapped it around me, covering the brown sack at my waist, before lying down on my side and sliding the scale behind my back, safely guarded between me and the wall.

Julie lay within my view. She met my gaze, and gave me a small smile. I returned the smile politely, then turned to face the other way, blocking her out and turning my thoughts to another girl. My girl. *River. Will I ever see her again?*

***

Since it would take seconds to travel to Uma's island, we left our camp as late afternoon approached. Our appointment was in the evening but Uma's sister had advised that we arrive a few hours earlier just in case.

When we arrived on the hilly island, the sky overhead was heavily overcast, so much so that not a ray of sun broke through the clouds and Bahir didn't need to use his powers to shelter Julie and me. We approached the doorstep of the castle. Before Arron could, I stepped forward and knocked on the heavy door.

Uma's sister opened the door promptly. Her round face lit up with recognition. "Aha. Come in, come in."

She swung the door wide open and allowed us all to step inside. She led us across the waiting room—now empty—and took a seat behind her desk. She opened up her ledger, and then glanced up at me. "So? Were you successful in acquiring the ingredients? I have noted down here you are due to pay a werewolf tooth, a strand of merflor, and a dragon scale."

"First, here's the dragon scale." I removed it from beneath my arm and handed it to her, watching with bated breath as she examined it.

Seemingly satisfied, she nodded and placed the item in a drawer. She looked up expectantly. "And then?"

I detached the brown sack from my belt and planted it down on the counter in front her. She loosened the string wrapped tightly around the opening and gazed down into the bag. She frowned.

"What?" I asked, my jaw tensing.

She pulled out the werewolf tooth. "This seems fine and genuine," she said, rolling the huge tooth in her palm. Her eyes flicked back up to me. "But I still need the merflor."

My stomach dropped. "What? It's in the bag…"

My voice trailed off as I snatched the bag from her and gazed down into it. It was empty.

*How?* I'd been examining the merflor just the day before yesterday.

*Could it have fallen out? What happened to it?*

*Could it have been removed?*

I spun around to face my companions. "Did one of you touch the merflor?"

Julie and Bahir looked blankly back at me. My eyes fell on Arron.

"Perhaps it fell out," he offered, furrowing his brows.

My eyes narrowed on him. I'd kept the bag tightly shut at all times. Even when we'd visited Breccan's cave, the sack had remained on my person and after we'd returned, the string had still been tied tightly around the opening.

*Could the Hawk be trying to jeopardize my meeting with the witch?*

I recalled the night before, when I'd been examining the merflor before returning it to the bag. That was the same night that Arron had approached me, handed me the vial of light blue liquid and made his "suggestion". That had also been the night Bahir had left me and I'd leapt from the cliff—possibly the only time that I'd been separated from the sack.

I'd felt the pain in my chest as Bahir prepared to exit. I'd dropped the sack before leaping from the mountain. Arron had remained on that ledge. He could have easily removed the light merflor and left only the tooth to provide some weight to the bag—so I wouldn't notice the merflor was missing until time ran out for our appointment.

There was no way I could prove any of this, and

perhaps it was just my frustration getting the better of me, but Arron had made no secret all along that his preference was to get rid of me rather than pursue a long-winded route of trying to cure me.

I cursed beneath my breath as I turned around to face Uma's sister again. She was tapping her fingers impatiently on the desk.

"Do you have the merflor or not?" she asked. "Because I'm afraid that without it, I can't give you an appointment."

"Just give me a moment, will you?" I said.

Grasping Arron by the shoulder, I pulled him across the room toward the door, Bahir and Julie following after me. I dragged him outside and, clutching his robe in my fists, pushed his back against the castle's rough wall. My eyes bored into his. "Are you quite certain you don't know where the merflor is?" I breathed.

He glared back at me. "Quite certain, vampire," he said coolly. "The last I saw of the plant was when you took it out and looked at it back at our camp."

My eyes continued to drill into his for several more

moments, trying to detect a faltering in his gaze, before letting him go.

I kicked the ground, spraying pebbles all around me. *Dammit.*

We needed to get some more merflor. But we were now only hours away from the time of my appointment. When Aisha had gone looking for it, it had taken her hours to find. Now that she knew where it was, it shouldn't take her too long to find again. Perhaps she could even procure it before the appointment. But we didn't have Aisha to help us any more. We had Bahir... Unless the male jinni felt that he had recovered enough to resume his hold on me.

I turned to Bahir. "How is your strength?" I asked. "Could you inhabit me again now?"

Doubt shrouded the jinni's strong-jawed face. "No, Benjamin," he said, shaking his head. "I can't risk it yet. I need more time... I haven't exactly been resting since I came out."

That much was true. I couldn't blame him, but it didn't lessen my frustration.

"Do you know where to find merflor in The

Cove?" I asked him, hoping desperately that he had a better idea of where it was than Aisha had when she'd first ventured down there.

"No," he said, dashing my hopes. "I would need to search for it."

I breathed out. *Oh, God.*

One thing was clear now—I would miss my appointment. I was going to have to try to push it back at least until tomorrow… and hope that the doctor wouldn't charge some kind of "postponement" fee.

I was about to turn on my heel and march back into the reception room to rearrange our appointment when Bahir let out a gasp, his body becoming rigid, eyes wide open. I froze, staring at him. His jaw slackened, his complexion growing pale. His eyes rolled in their sockets, then fixed somewhere above my head, as though he was seeing and also not seeing.

"Bahir?" I breathed, stepping toward him. "What's wrong?"

My words snapped him out of whatever trance he

had just fallen into. He rushed forward and grabbed my arms, sheer terror in his eyes. His lips parted, his breathing quickened. "Nuriya," he said in a choked whisper. "S-She needs me. She is… in grave danger. I-I must go!"

Panic surged through me. "What? No! You can't—!"

But he did.

I could barely believe my eyes, but a second later, the jinni had vanished from the spot.

# CHAPTER 26: BEN

*What just happened?*

I was in a state of shock.

It took a few moments for reality to sink in as I stared dumbfounded at the spot where Bahir had just disappeared.

He'd abandoned us. Just like that.

My thumb reached for the golden band around my wrist and brushed against the snake's head.

*No. He has to come back. He has to come back.*

I pressed against the band of gold harder than I'd

ever done before, so hard that the snake's head bent out of shape. I kept expecting him to come back, or if not him, some other jinni. But nobody came. And of course Aisha was stuck inside me staving off the Elder—I couldn't afford for her to come out for even a moment.

*What did he mean, Nuriya is in danger? And how can he just abandon his duty to me like this?*

I could only think that something had gone terribly wrong back in The Oasis. What, I couldn't imagine.

*And what now? How will we get through this without a jinni by our side?*

"No!" I exhaled in frustration. I left the castle and raced down the hill toward the shore. Toward the direction I supposed the jinni had headed. However futile it was, I couldn't think of anything else to do in that moment but run. I had been so accepting of the idea that a second jinni would remain assisting me as long as I needed. Now that he'd gone, my mind spiraled into a panic.

I reached the bottom of the cliff, arriving at the

beach. I stared out at the endless mass of water surrounding us. I breathed in deeply, trying to calm my racing pulse, even as I continued to touch the twisted snake head.

*Think. Just think. There has to be a way out of this. There just has to.*

I was too preoccupied to notice the speeding footsteps behind me until they arrived so close I could no longer ignore them. When I spun around, it was to see Arron, brandishing a sharp iron rod, aimed directly at my chest.

"No!" Julie's shout came from my right.

I barely had time to react when she shot into Arron's side like a missile, flooring him. Before I could even come to my senses enough to yell for her to stop, Julie had wrestled the rod out of the Hawk's hand. Hurling it aside, she extended her claws and slit right across Arron's throat.

"No!" I bellowed, lunging forward and hauling her off the Hawk.

But it was too late. Far too late. She'd plunged her claws so deep that they had severed his jugular.

I turned on her, shocked.

"Y-You killed him!" I hissed.

Her lips trembled as she gasped, "He was going to murder you! I suspected he was waiting for this moment all along—for you to be without a jinni by your side. He would have gouged your heart out! I didn't know what else to do." Her voice rose to hysteria as she clasped a bloody hand to her mouth.

I looked back down at Arron's body. He, the great leader of the Hawks, who had once stricken fear in the heart of all vampires, now a bloodied corpse in the sand.

I still hadn't wrapped my mind around the fact that Bahir had left us, and now here I was: two of my most useful companions lost within the space of a few minutes.

*God help me.*

My gaze shifted back to the shell-shocked vampire.

*Now it's just me… and this girl.*

# Chapter 27: Ben

I didn't have even the slightest clue of what was to happen now. What would become of me. I continued rubbing the gold band, but it was to no avail.

"Benjamin," Julie said in a quiet voice. "I think we should get rid of Arron's corpse. I don't know how the witch sisters would react if they found out that we had murdered someone on their property. Arron even seemed to have some kind of connection to them."

She was right. The two of us bent down over the Hawk—me clutching his shoulders while Julie held his feet—and dragged him into the waves. We swam deep enough for the current to begin carrying him away. We returned to the beach and approached the bloodstained patch of sand where the Hawk had lain. I dug my heels in deep and unearthed the sand, kicking it about until the bloodstains were less detectable. When the tide came in, it would wash over it anyway.

I dipped down to the water and splashed my face—even though it was already wet—as if it would bring me some semblance of clarity.

One thing was for certain: I had to give up hope of having the heart surgery now. There was no way Julie and I would be able to procure the merflor, which meant that there would be no chance the witch doctor would see us—her sister had already made that amply clear. And, heck, I didn't even have the first clue about how we were going to get off this tiny island.

"What are you thinking?" Julie asked.

I shook my head. "I don't know." I looked down into her wide hazel eyes.

She wet her lower lip. "The witch might not be of any help to us now in having lost the merflor, but… she must have a boat on this island that we could take."

"And go where?" I said, my voice strained.

Julie hesitated again. "Maybe we should go to my father… The box," she murmured.

*Oh, joy. The Elder box-trap thing.*

I would've let out a bitter laugh had I not been so devastated. Her suggestion had just signified my entrance into depths of desperation that even I hadn't believed I would be forced to plunge into.

Even if somehow, Julie's idea worked, how would we reach her father now that we had no jinni to transport us? My hunger pangs were growing stronger by the hour. Soon, they would be unbearable.

I didn't have days to spend sailing the seas in search of Julie's father's ship. Besides, I didn't know how long Aisha would be able to last in me. I didn't know if she would last as long as Bahir, whether she possessed even half as much stamina as him. And once she came out, that would be the beginning of the end.

Julie drew in a sharp breath. "Look, Benjamin," she said. "Whether or not we look for the box, or think of something else, we can't just stay here on this island."

"And where exactly is this island anyway?" I said. "Even if we were going to go looking for your father—whom you suspect is hovering around The Tavern somewhere—we don't even know where we are. I have no idea how to navigate seas in this supernatural dimension."

"I've spent nearly twenty years at sea," Julie replied. "I know something about navigating these waters... Though I do need to know the exact location of this place."

"And even if we managed to find your father's ship in time, how would we get the box?" I asked. "We have no jinni available to airlift it."

Julie drew in a deep breath. "I... I could return to my father," she said, her voice low with resignation.

That made me pause.

"Return to your father?" I asked. "What do you

mean?"

"I mean, I would go back to him." She lowered her eyes to the ground. "There'd be no other way to get the box to you. It's in my father's study—which is usually locked—right at the base of the ship, so even if I managed to slip on board without anybody noticing and enter my father's study, I wouldn't be able to get off the ship without being spotted lugging a huge box... I've thought about it," she said, more firmly this time. "Helping you is more important than my escape from my father."

I stared at her, surprised that she would be willing to do this for me. Then I reminded myself for the umpteenth time that this was not just for me—this was for the safety of all realms. The Elders' resurgence would affect all vampires, humans, and God knew how many other species now that the Hawks were no longer a strong enough force to keep the Elders restrained.

"Just wait here," Julie said. "I'll go back up to the castle and try to find out from Uma's sister exactly where we are. The situation might not be as bad as we think. For all we know, we could be close to The Tavern."

The former I found hard to believe, but I let Julie leave, watching as she scurried up the hill toward the stone building at the top.

Alone now—or as alone as I could be with two supernaturals fighting a war inside of me—I fixed my gaze back out on the ocean. The sky was still overcast, thank God. Without a jinni, Julie and I would've been roasted by now.

Wanting to take my mind off the hollow feeling in my stomach as I waited for the vampire to return, I started running further up the shoreline to look for any kind of vessel that we could use to leave this island. The main problem with Julie's suggestion was that finding the box was only half of the battle. Even if she managed to get her father to hand it over to me, or somehow swiped it for me in some other way, then what? I'd have to travel to Cruor in order to be close enough to trap Basilius—the very place that I had been fighting tooth and nail to stay away from.

I shook myself. *I need to stop trying to think so far*

*ahead. Just one step at a time, or I will drive myself insane.*

Whatever we decided to do, Julie was right that we could not just stay on this island. We had to keep moving. I sped up and reached the end of the current stretch of beach, arriving before a large cluster of boulders. I was about to lay my hands on the rock nearest me and clamber over the cluster to continue my search for a suitable boat to escape in when a familiar female voice spoke behind me.

"Benjamin Novak."

I spun around. My jaw dropped to the floor as I found myself face to face with... "Hortencia?"

The small, fragile young woman, clad in a long dark robe, stood quite still before me, a silver visor covering the fleshy pits where her eyes should've been. Her lips were clamped tightly shut.

"What are you doing here?" I asked, dumbfounded.

She reached up a hand and, with curved forefinger, beckoned me closer. I took a step forward. She gripped the front of my cloak, yanking me nearer still. She tilted her head upward as if to look me in the eyes, if she possessed them herself.

Her lips unglued from the hard line they had formed. "Something's happened," she said in a quiet voice. "Something that has never happened before."

She paused, leaving me hanging.

"What?" I urged.

"My sister and I… our eyes have diverged." She let go of my robe and her small palms flattened against my chest, directly over my heart. "Although we are twins, my sister Pythia and I differ in a number of ways. However, never before have our eyes not seen as one. She envisioned a different path for you than I did, vampire."

Again Hortencia paused, infuriatingly. I gripped her shoulders and shook her.

"What did she envision?"

"I would not suggest that my eye is more accurate than my sister's," she continued as though she hadn't heard me. "Thus, I can only conclude that fate has carved out two paths for you." Her hands slipped beneath my cloak and then through my ripped shirt, settling directly over flesh. Her fingers felt moist and clammy. The strange black symbols tattooed up her neck began to swirl and migrate around the center of her throat.

"Since earlier today, one of your feet is already over the edge. You are on the verge of being faced with a decision. It will happen soon. Very soon. Whichever path you choose will determine your true identity, and your place in the history of the universe." Her face tensed, her voice strained as she parted her cracked lips and hissed, "When the road forks, your route will be clear. Either a destroyer or hero of realms you shall be."

To my horror, her hands slipped away from my chest, and she jolted backward.

"No!" I lurched forward, reaching out to grab her, but it was too late. She disappeared before I could latch on to her. "No!" I yelled again.

*Destroyer or hero of realms? What does that actually mean?*

*What did she mean when she said one foot was already over the edge? The loss of a jinni and the demise of Arron?*

*But she said I had a choice.*

As desperate and hopeless as the situation was, those words shone a light. Ever since my visit to the oracle's cave, I'd feared at the back of my mind that she was right. That my destiny indeed was to become a soldier of shadows and be lost to the Elders, their slave in helping them come to resurgence. The fact that Hortencia herself had said that her sister— wherever and whoever she was—had seen a different future for me, one where I could be a hero rather than a destroyer, sparked an unexpected ray of hope in me.

But how would this play out? And, dammit, why couldn't she have stayed a few moments longer to help me? Wouldn't the rise of the Elders affect her too? She was part jinni, part witch. She held magic. She could've easily stayed and at the very least transported Julie and me to our next destination, even if she refused to give us any more information. Would that have hurt her so much?

There was no point in lamenting what was out of

reach. She was gone and I was on my own again. Although at least I was now armed with confirmation that there could be another way.

I remained still, watching the spot where the oracle had vanished, but soon it was clear she wouldn't be returning. I turned around and clambered up the boulders, continuing my search for a boat. Her visit hadn't changed our immediate plans. We still had to get off this island, and I still had to figure out if I really was going to go through with Julie's suggestion.

As I reached the other side of the boulders, I was glad to see a small harbor filled with a dozen boats. To my surprise, Julie was also standing on the bay, accompanied by the redheaded witch.

I hung back, watching as Uma's sister pointed toward one of the boats—a small yet sturdy-looking vessel with a narrow covering over the bow. I didn't know exactly what kind of negotiation Julie was coming to with the witch, so I figured it was best I didn't interrupt. I kept my distance until the witch had left Julie's side and vanished herself, presumably back to the castle.

I ran over to Julie. Her eyes widened as she spotted me.

"Ben," she said, stepping down from the boat and onto the wooden floorboards of the jetty. "I was about to come and get you."

"What's happening?" I asked, deciding not to tell Julie about the oracle's visit to me just now. There was no point. It wasn't like Hortencia had offered a single shred of practical information that could help us in our predicament. Besides, the exchange I'd had with Hortencia somehow felt too personal to share with Julie.

"I managed to strike a deal with the witch," Julie said. "Even though she was adamant that you could not receive treatment without the third ingredient, I told her that she and her sister could keep the two ingredients that we brought with us—the werewolf tooth and the dragon scale—on the condition that they provided us with a boat as well as a sea chart and directions on how to reach The Tavern. It seems you still haven't decided for sure whether you want to pursue my father's ship, but at least if we arrive in the waters near The Tavern, we will be in a more familiar place." She climbed back onto the boat and headed toward the bow. "I did, of course, at first try to bargain with the witch to transport us to our next destination by magic, but she wouldn't agree to it. So this was the best deal I could come to."

"Did you ask if she knew of any other doctors who can treat a vampire?"

"I did ask if there was anyone else in the supernatural world who could perform the operation for you, but the witch was tightlipped, as is to be expected, I guess. I don't see why she'd recommend another doctor even if she knew of them. She told me that there was only her sister who specialized in such treatments. It could've been a lie, but we have no way of knowing. Even Arron suggested that this witch Uma was one of a kind in her medical skill and knowledge, and more importantly, in her willingness to treat non-witches."

*Some willingness,* I thought bitterly

I climbed onto the boat and walked to the bow. As with all the other boats I had seen so far in this supernatural dimension, this one was also drawn by sea creatures—two large, pure white dolphins, to be precise. Their reins hung over a metal clamp, behind which was a wooden bench just about wide enough for the two of us to sit.

"Okay." I breathed out, looking back up at the sky—still mercifully swarming with clouds. At least there was a small covering we could take shelter under once the sun broke through. "This boat should be all right, I guess."

"So..." Julie began tentatively after a pause. "Where exactly are we headed?"

As much as it made my stomach sink, I couldn't think of any way to reply other than, "Let's head for your father's ship."

Maybe by some miracle along the way we'd come up with some other idea. But for now, this was all I had.

Julie nodded and immediately grabbed the reins, taking a seat on the bench. I walked to the stern of the ship and stood gripping the railing, the wind blasting through my hair as the dolphins lurched forward with supernatural speed. I watched the witches' hilly island grow further and further away.

All the while, Hortencia's words played over in my mind.

*"Either a destroyer or hero of realms you shall be."*

# Chapter 28: Ben

I didn't know how many miles an hour we were traveling, but these dolphins were anything but ordinary. Uma's island soon turned into a dot the size of a period until it faded completely out of view. We found ourselves entering a world of endless masses of water. The waves were calm at least, which I was glad for. The speed at which the dolphins were traveling made the ride bumpy enough.

As expected, the clouds didn't keep the sun at bay for long. They began to thin, allowing rays of piercing sunshine to spill down from the heavens. So much so that it became uncomfortable for the two of us even while sitting beneath the covering. It wasn't very wide, and sunshine kept spilling onto us, even when we sat directly in the middle of it. My only relief came from Julie's confidence in navigating the boat. She constantly consulted a map and by the time night descended, she assured me that she recognized the area we'd reached. This was the hope I clung to, even as the hours passed by. Precious hours. Hours that, for all I knew, could be the last of my life. At least, a life worth living.

I was grateful to Julie that she insisted that she didn't need to sleep, hence we didn't waste any more time. The dolphins were showing no signs of tiring, although I supposed we would have to stop at some point for them to feed. Hopefully that would not take long and we could continue traveling throughout the night.

Julie and I barely spoke, even as we sat so close to each other, we were practically touching due to the narrowness of the bench. But as night progressed, she became more talkative.

"I'm thinking about how exactly we will do this," she said, her eyes fixed on the waves. "Once we spot my father's boat, I will bring ours right up to it. I'll board it first and seek out my father. Once I've brought the box upstairs, you probably need to step aboard at least for a few moments to help transfer the box to your boat. It's large and even though I could manage its weight, my arms aren't physically long enough to lower it..." She threw me a sideways glance. "You need not worry about being in danger from my father's crew. You won't stay long and they'll all be too preoccupied with my return to pay much attention to you."

"What makes you think he'll give up the box so easily?" I asked, frowning.

"I never said that it would be easy," she said, tightening her hold on the reins. "But I know my father... Somehow, I'll find a way to get it to you. That is my worry, not yours. You have enough to worry about as it is."

"And then how will I get to Cruor?" Asking the

question sent chills running down my spine.

Her jaw tensed. "That is, I'm afraid, something that I cannot help you with," she said, to my dismay. "But you'll have the box on your boat. Despite the distance from The Tavern area to Cruor, it's a straightforward journey, and there are a number of landmarks along the way. I'll leave this map with you and tell you which signs to look out for."

"And human blood," I muttered. "You said some needs to be placed inside it?"

"Yes," she said. "Human blood is something I can help you with. We have a small stock of it on board my father's ship—or at least we did when I left. I'm sure it's still there and I'd manage to swipe enough for you without too much difficulty. Once we get the box, I'll give you detailed instructions and advice, as much as I remember the warlock giving my father. It's hard to explain thoroughly without having it in front of us."

She paused, falling silent for a while. When she spoke again, her voice was lower. "Once I return to my father, it won't be so simple to extricate myself again. It pains me to think of you alone in this. Though in fact... I'll be sad to leave you at all." She left her words hanging in the air as I wondered what exactly she meant by them. Then her glance, infused with an unexpected affection, made me realize.

"I... I would have liked to have known you better," she continued. "I guess what I'm saying is, men like you don't grow on trees."

She smiled to herself bitterly. I wondered if she was thinking of her fiancé, the man she was so opposed to marrying that she would rather risk her life escaping. The man her father would surely force her to accept once she returned.

There was an awkward silence, as I had no idea how to respond. I had too much weighing on my mind to be able to think much about her apparent attachment for me. Even if I hadn't, River held my heart. Every part of it. As attractive and kind as Julie seemed to be, she couldn't hold a candle to the girl I'd professed my love to. I didn't want to hurt the vampire either, however. Not after all she'd done to help me.

I realized that I hadn't mentioned River until now. Perhaps because the thought of saying her name out loud was painful, since there was a strong chance that I would never see her again.

But I didn't want to give Julie any kind of false hope. Hope that, even if I did manage to survive all this, I might have some attraction for her, and find a way to cross paths with her again in the future. I had to crush that now, for her sake.

"Julie," I said, looking sincerely into her eyes. "Thank you. You've helped me through what has been the most desperate time of my life. I'll be forever grateful to you. But I need to tell you that I have a girlfriend, back in The Shade." I'd thought that talking about River would be painful, but somehow, it was strangely cathartic, and so I continued. "Her name is River Giovanni. I'm in love with her. Deeply, madly in love with her."

To my surprise, Julie responded with a smile. "Oh, I know about River."

I cocked my head to one side. "What?"

Her smile widened and she looked fondly at me. "I

heard you mention her the other day, when we were camping outside the dragon's cave... I'm pretty sure you fell asleep for a bit, or at least dozed off into semi-consciousness. You were breathing her name. I figured she must be someone you care deeply about."

I hadn't realized that I'd managed to fall so deeply into rest, much less that I'd been so audible about what was on my mind.

Our conversation became a bit stilted after that. I stood up and, it being dark now, I walked freely around the deck and stretched my legs.

I remained at a distance from Julie for the next few hours, watching the waves froth and foam. All the while, I tried to ignore my increasing hunger. As the early hours of morning approached, I felt a very different sensation within the pit of my stomach. A more worrying sensation. Like the pangs of hunger, it was painful, but this pain was more intense, more acute. As if someone was drilling a nail through me. I recognized it as the beginnings of the same sensation I'd experienced just before Bahir had left me. Before I'd leapt from the cliff. Before the Elder had regained control over my mind.

*Is Aisha tiring already?* This was what I'd feared. That she might be weaker than the other jinni and unable to last as long. I shut my eyes tight, summoning every ounce of willpower I possessed, as though willing alone would force Aisha to remain within me.

*She can't leave me now. Not yet.*

My fists clenched around the iron railing. I found myself squeezing so tightly that the metal bent out of shape. I held my breath, bracing myself for the pain to worsen. But to my surprise, after perhaps five minutes, it died down. I breathed out a slow sigh of relief.

*Perhaps it's not a sign of her weakening after all. Maybe that was just a temporary glitch. Aisha not paying attention, or something...* I prayed that it was true. Everything rested on this jinni. This girl who had so aggravated me on first meeting now held my life in her hands. Her stamina and will to help me was the only thing keeping my head above water.

Swallowing hard, I left my spot and moved back

toward the bench where Julie sat.

"I have good news," she said, sensing me approach.

*Good news.* The notion was foreign to me.

"What?" I asked, resuming my seat next to her.

She nodded straight ahead. I looked out toward the ocean and spotted the outline of an island.

"That's The Tavern," she said. "Uma's island wasn't so far at all."

I hadn't expected the journey to go so smoothly. We hadn't even stopped to let the dolphins feed yet. I felt almost suspicious of this stroke of good luck.

"And now… your father's ship?" I said. "Where do you think that is?"

"We need to sail around a bit more and try to find it," she replied, speeding the dolphins forward.

We traveled closer to the island, and then we began to move around it. By the time we'd reached three quarters of the way around its circumference, I'd spotted a ship in the distance. Of course, The Tavern was a hub for supernatural creatures, and large ships in these waters ought to have been an everyday occurrence. And yet…

I pointed toward it.

"Oh, my," Julie said in a hushed tone. She stood up and peered out over the dark waters toward the looming vessel. "That's it. That's my father's ship. I was right that he would still be in this area." Nervousness filled Julie's face as she tightened her grip on the reins. She gulped, her breathing growing more uneven.

I felt bad for her being forced to return to what she'd described as a miserable and downtrodden existence, but there wasn't anything else I could suggest. She'd made this decision herself and the only thing that I could think to do was thank her, which I'd already done a number of times.

The ship was anchored and dark. Not a single light shone through the windows. Julie's nerves were almost palpable as we arrived right at the base of the ship. She pulled the dolphins to a stop, and then wrapped the reins securely around the metal post in front of her seat.

She glanced up at me, and gave me a small nod.

"Okay," she said in a quiet voice. "I-I'm going to

board the ship… I will first attempt to get to the box without waking anyone or my father knowing, but I'm sure that will be impossible for the reasons I already described."

I had no idea how she was planning to convince her father to part with such a supposedly rare and valuable item, especially after she had betrayed him and run away. But she seemed confident that she could find a way to pull it off, so all I could do was trust her.

Her gaze remained on me for a few moments before she backed away. Moving to the bow of our boat, she took a giant leap and latched onto the railing lining the deck of the tall ship. She swung her legs over and disappeared from sight.

That left me waiting in excruciating silence. I took up the reins, worried that the dolphins might go lunging forward for some reason. My eyes traveled toward the front of Mr. Duan's ship. Dozens of ropes hung down the front of it—reins—and submerged in the water. I wondered what sea creatures drove this huge ship forward. Hopefully not something that could aggravate the two dolphins. Thankfully, they remained quite still.

I doubled over as an intense pain fired through my chest. The same disconcerting pain that I'd prayed was a one-off. Now I couldn't push away the doubt that this was more than just a temporary lack of Aisha's concentration or a slip-up. She was becoming tired, I could sense it.

*Aisha, you've got to hold on.* I willed that she could hear me.

"Benjamin."

Julie's hushed voice called down from the deck of the ship. I looked up with both relief and surprise. I hadn't expected her back nearly so soon. Perhaps she'd managed to get the box without her father waking up after all, or perhaps the ship was empty.

Though it turned out that neither was the case.

She beckoned me to jump up to her. "You can come now," she whispered. "I'll explain. Just leave the dolphins where they are. Don't worry, they won't go anywhere."

I double-checked that the reins were secure before

leaping up to her. When I arrived on the deck, I expected it to be empty—especially from the way that Julie had been whispering to me. I certainly wasn't expecting to see four vampires standing behind Julie in a semi-circle.

I looked with uncertainty from one to the other. Three men and one woman. They were all young, perhaps a year or two apart in age. Their skin was whiter than Julie's, and each possessed distinctly European features.

I didn't get much further into wondering who these people were exactly, as the young man standing directly in front of me whipped out a thin tubular object, placed it against his mouth, and released a breath.

The next thing I knew, a sharp object had buried itself into my neck. A burning sensation erupted around it. My head felt light and I fell to my knees. Dizziness overtook me as the half-circle of vampires closed in around me. Hands forced my back against the floor and closed around my ankles, hands, and shoulders. I was lifted from the ground. My sight and awareness were fading fast, but I was still conscious enough to feel my limbs knock against hard edges, my body placed in some kind of narrow trunk.

As I gazed upward through foggy vision, it was Julie who stared down at me, expressionless. Her hands moved to the lid of the container and she lowered it down slowly over me until all faded to black.

# Chapter 29: Ben

I woke to a cool wind blowing against my face. My eyelids felt heavy as lead. I became keenly aware of the throbbing pain in my neck. My muscles felt strained and torn, as though I'd been put through a shredder. As I tried to move my legs, they knocked against hard walls either side of me.

When I forced my eyes open, my misted vision cleared, giving way to the sight of... Aisha.

She crouched over me. Her lips were puckered, and I realized that she'd been blowing on me. Panic gleamed in her eyes and she looked drained and exhausted.

"Benjamin!" she whispered. "We're trapped!"

I tried to distance myself from the jinni, but there simply wasn't enough room. I couldn't sit up fully, but I sat up as much as I could, while Aisha slid down my legs, giving me some breathing space.

"What happened?" I asked. Although my vision had cleared, my mind was still in a fog.

"I don't know," she hissed. "I couldn't stay in you any longer. The Elder sucked too much out of me. I was forced to emerge, and when I did we were both trapped in... this? What is this?" Her voice rose to soprano. "I'm a jinni. I can move through walls. Why can't I penetrate this box?"

*This box.*

The words triggered something and slowly, the pieces began to fall into place. My head reeled as my last memory came back to me. Julie, closing the lid of this... this box.

Her Elder trap.

The sheer magnitude of her betrayal hit me full

force. *All that time...* I wondered when exactly it had started. Had it been after she'd found out what I was capable of unleashing? Had she seen me as the threat that I was, just as Arron had? Unlike the Hawk, she'd gained my trust. Was her motive truly the same as Arron's? She had been opposed to the surgery from the start, and instead had proposed her box idea. The box that held the power to trap an Elder. Apparently also capable of trapping a jinni.

Had Julie been planning to finish me off all along? But too many things about this simply didn't make sense. If this had been her plan, why hadn't she teamed up with the Hawk? Why had she killed him when he had attempted to stake me? She should have just hung back and watched as he aimed the iron rod right through my chest. Why had she helped me in the dragon cave? And why hadn't she attempted to kill me herself already, when she'd had more than enough opportunity?

None of it made any sense. And besides these inconsistencies, she had seemed so genuine... So... helpless. I couldn't help but wonder whether any of her story was true at all—whether she was indeed on the run from her father. But then who were those men who'd come after her, the ones I'd ended up killing? Perhaps that part of the story was true, and it was only once she'd found out that I was marked by an Elder that she'd changed her plans, deciding that getting rid of me was more important than running from her father. Her words rang in my ears. *"Helping you is more important than my escape from my father."*

Had she meant that getting rid of me was more important? But then why hadn't she? Why lock me in this box? Why keep me alive for another moment knowing the destruction that I was capable of causing?

"Where are we, Ben?" Aisha asked, her voice shaking. "You must know where we are." She grabbed my hand and shook it.

Before I could answer her, the obvious hit me.

"Aisha," I breathed, gaping at the jinni. "You... You've left me. How..." My voice trailed off. *How am I still myself?* The twisting pain that I'd felt earlier when I'd feared that Aisha was on her way out... I could no longer feel that. Although the hunger pangs remained, I was sensing no signs of the Elder taking control.

*What is happening?*

Aisha continued to harass me with questions, but I still had too many of my own to come up with a single answer.

*Could it be that this box separates me from the influence of the Elder? That, although he has bored a connection between the two of us deep within my heart, being in this box means that his influence cannot reach me?*

If what Julie had told me was true—and it seemed true to me based on the jinni's inability to escape—this box could contain subtle beings. Beings who weren't of flesh and bone. And while I was inside it, these walls would serve as barriers to the Elder's influence reaching me.

My mind churned, my doubts swinging in another direction. What if locking me in here was Julie doing me a favor? Cutting me off from the Elder.

But then why not make the suggestion to me

herself? Why shut me in here in such a backhanded manner?

Aisha's desperation boiled over the edge. She clutched my throat and shook me hard. "What's going on, Ben?"

I had to attempt to answer her questions. Gripping her hands, I shoved them away from my neck and tried to form a coherent sentence.

"First of all, I don't know exactly what happened," I said, my voice hoarse. My mind traveled back to the last time Aisha had seen the light of day—back on Breccan's island. "After Bahir left me, we managed to get the dragon scale. Then we headed back to Uma's island, but I couldn't get an appointment with the witch because somehow we had lost the merflor. I suspected Arron of taking it…"

Now my trust in Julie had been shaken, I wondered whether it could've been her who had removed the merflor from the sack. From the very start she had been vocal about her doubts about the surgery and made it clear that she thought we ought to find some other way.

I tried to think how she could have taken the merflor. I recalled the night Bahir had left me and the Elder had overtaken me. Before leaping from the cliff, I'd dropped the sack. In the blur of confusion that must have followed my leap, Julie could have found a way to remove the plant, perhaps flinging it over the cliffside. The others being preoccupied, I supposed it wouldn't have been that difficult to do it without anyone noticing.

Even still, I couldn't place a finger on exactly what her motive would've been for me to not have the surgery. If she had locked me in this box because she wanted to somehow save me from the Elder's influence rather than destroy me as Arron had wanted, why was she so against my being cured by a different method? That surgery, if successful, would have brought me a permanent cure. I couldn't remain in this box forever... Could I?

Aisha shook me again. "Ben!" she hissed. "What happened after you found out that you were missing the merflor?"

I fought to refocus my addled brain. "Then...

Then Bahir left altogether," I said. "He just took off."

Aisha's eyes bulged. "What?" she gasped. "Why? How could he have just left you?"

"I don't know," I said. "He said something about Nuriya being in grave danger. He just said that he had to go. Using my wrist band, I tried to summon him back, or summon another jinni to me, but nobody came."

The jinni's hands clamped over her mouth. "Oh, no! No! I can't believe this could have happened."

"That what could have happened?" I asked.

"I can only think of one thing that would cause Nuriya to be in such danger that Bahir would abandon you. The one thing that caused her to flee to The Oasis in the first place."

Now it was me who was shaking her. "Flee from what?"

"The Drizan jinn," Aisha breathed, her eyes wide with terror. "They must've found her. Found us. I can't think how else—"

"The Drizan jinn? Who are they?"

She hesitated, doubt filling her face, as though

wondering whether she really ought to answer my question. But she'd spilled so much already, it didn't make sense for her not to continue.

"What?" I urged.

"Do you remember the first day we met… before lunch?" she asked. "I slipped up and said something that I shouldn't have. From the look in your eyes, you noticed."

I nodded. I remembered. She had hinted that one of the reasons they kept themselves hidden in an atrium so low beneath the ground was that they would be the last to be reached in a raid.

"Well," she continued, "the Drizan are the ones who would raid us if they ever found out our location…" Her eyebrows knotted in a deep frown. "But how would they find out about us?"

I of course had no idea. But this wasn't the most pressing question on my mind.

"I need to get out of here!" she shrilled. She attacked the lid of the container, but it remained unbudged. I had half a mind to help her, but this box was the only thing keeping me from dashing off the ship and plunging into the ocean on a deranged quest to reach Cruor.

I gripped the jinni's arms. "Wait," I said, even though I'd realized by now she would never get out no matter how hard she tried. "We need to think."

Tears seeped from her amethyst eyes and rolled down her full cheeks. She brushed them aside, trying to recompose herself. "Tell me what happened after Bahir left," she choked.

"Arron tried to murder me," I replied.

Aisha gasped.

"Julie stopped him, and killed him instead. Then..." Hortencia's visit played in my mind. I decided to skip over that part. Again it felt like the words she spoke were meant for me and me alone. "Then Julie and I managed to find a boat, and she brought me to her father's ship... where she and a group of other vampires locked me in this box." From the slight rocking, I guessed that we were still on the ship.

"Why would you follow her to her father's ship?" Aisha asked.

I explained in brief what Julie had told me about the box, and how I could see no other options than to take up her suggestion.

"An Elder trap?" Aisha murmured, a mixture of horror and fascination in her eyes as she gazed around the box. "How did they even create this thing?"

"Julie said that it was a gift from a warlock. Though she didn't seem to know who initially created it."

Aisha gazed at me, her soft, youthful features marred with fear. "And what now, Benjamin? What is to become of us?'

"I don't know, Aisha," I said heavily. "I don't know."

# CHAPTER 30: BEN

Hours passed. All Aisha and I could do was wait and hope, however feebly, that somehow the situation wasn't as bad as it seemed. That we would discover a silver lining. That Julie was not my enemy.

The ship seemed to enter a rough patch. The to-ing and fro-ing of the vessel rocked Aisha and me from side to side in the narrow box. Perhaps we'd entered a storm. A storm that appeared to be getting worse. Soon I had to exert myself just to keep my head from banging against the hard walls.

Then came a jolt. My forehead smashed against the roof of the box. It felt like the vessel had just come to an abrupt stop.

I heard footsteps. It sounded like those of several people coming from above. It seemed that we were being kept on a lower deck. The footsteps drew closer and louder as they thudded down what sounded like a staircase. They reached the rim of the box and stopped.

I held my breath, wondering if they were going to open the lid. They didn't. Instead, the box was hoisted upward and we were carried until we reached what I guessed was a flight of stairs. The box tilted, and since I had nothing to hold on to, my feet almost went slamming into Aisha, who was curled up on the other side. Once the stairs were climbed, the box leveled again. The footsteps continued beneath us as we were carried forward. Now, the sound of waves was more pronounced. Perhaps we had arrived on the uppermost deck.

*Where are they taking us?*

I caught the sound of a bolt being drawn, and the

creaking of heavy wood followed by a dull thud. Once again the box was tilted, but this time it felt like we were being carried down a smooth ramp, rather than bumpy stairs.

"Where are we going?" Aisha yelled through the box.

She received no answer.

We reached the end of the slope they were traveling down. Stones crunched beneath their feet and then the ride got bumpy again. So bumpy that I had to flatten my palms against the sides of the walls and push outward to stop my head from crashing against the lid again. It felt like they were climbing over… rocks? They sped up, making the journey only more uncomfortable.

"What are they going to do with us?" Aisha murmured, I suspected more to herself than to me.

Our carriers stopped abruptly. They lowered the box. The floor shuddered beneath me as we were planted down on the ground.

I held my breath, straining my ears to catch any clues as to where we were. The waves sounded distant now, so distant that they were but a far-off whisper. None of our carriers spoke. All I could hear was the scratching of stones beneath their feet.

Before I could realize what was happening, the wall of the box that my head rested against gave way. Strong hands slipped inside and clutched my elbows, jerking me out of the oblong container. My back scraped against rough ground. There was a snap. My eyes shot to my feet just in time to see the side door close again—a side door in the box that I hadn't even realized existed. They'd acted so fast and unexpectedly that Aisha hadn't had a chance to slip out.

Five faces stared down at me, including Julie's— directly above me. They gathered in a tight circle around me, so much so that I couldn't see where we were. All I knew was that I was lying on a rocky surface, it was cold, and it was dim.

I motioned to leap to my feet when one of the male vampires—the same one who'd shot a tranquilizer dart into my neck—whipped out a needle and thrust it into my right ankle.

"No!" I hissed, kicking him aside. My foot made contact with his leg, just above his knee. The crack of bone pierced the air and he yelped, stumbling backward. But it was too late. Whatever substance he'd just injected into me was acting fast. My legs lost their feeling even as I tried desperately to stand up. They became paralyzed. Julie dipped down suddenly, pulling out a black sack from her robe.

I extended my claws and swiped upward. She dodged and whispered to the others, "Restrain his arms." As the three vampires left grabbed hold of my arms and fought to press them to the ground, Julie forced my head upward and slipped the sack over it, blocking my vision.

"No!" I growled.

I was lifted once again, even as I continued to struggle and swipe. They carried me away from the box. Although my vision was gone, it became clearer than ever that they were climbing up a slope.

And then they stopped.

"Here," Julie said.

They lowered me to the ground. Although my legs

were still motionless, at least my arms were unhindered by their grasp. I reached up and removed the sack, able to take in my surroundings for the first time as the vampires stepped out of reach of my claws.

My heart skipped a beat. I forgot how to breathe as I took in a chillingly familiar sight.

The sky was shrouded with dark, murky clouds and tinged with an eerie, crimson hue. There was a complete absence of vegetation and sprawling all around me were black mountains with peaks as pointed as knives. I lay beneath one such peak, on a cluster of level rocks. A few feet away from me, the ground dipped. I propped myself up with my hands to glimpse a wide, black hole in the ground. A crater.

I'd seen this before.

I'd been here before.

This was the place of my first vision. The place Arron's traitor wife had brought me as an infant. The place where the Elder had first left his mark on me. And now, where the Elder would reclaim me.

I twisted back to face the vampires who'd carried me here. My eyes locked with Julie's. Her gaze was no longer stoic as I'd expected it to be—rather, there was almost a trace of… guilt? Regret?

"I'm sorry," she mouthed. Her eyes lingered on me for several more seconds before she turned on her heel and raced away with the other vampires, disappearing from view over the edge of the mountain. Their footsteps echoed as they clambered down the rocks, fading into the distance.

My eyes traveled back to the crater.

It hit me only now that even though I was no longer in the box and I was unprotected by any jinni, I still didn't feel the Elder rising up within me to take over my mind. I realized why. He had no more need to beckon me back to Cruor. I'd already arrived.

I couldn't even begin to imagine why Julie would deliver me to the Elder's doorstep when she knew what it would mean. Why she was on the Elder's side, and apparently working for him all along. What she could possibly stand to gain from it. But it didn't matter. I was here.

An icy wind swept up from nowhere.

"Benjamin." Goosebumps ran along my skin as a

low whisper echoed up from the crevice. Faint at first, as though it traveled up from the deepest chambers of the mountain. But gradually, it grew louder. And louder.

Even the parts of my body that weren't paralyzed froze as the whisper drew nearer.

A crimson mist formed above the crater. The whisper no longer echoed. It hissed straight into my ears, as though just feet away from me. The reddish mist thickened and turned black. The chilling voice stopped repeating my name and instead said, "Welcome back."

So this was where my journey had led me.

Hortencia's initial prediction had been accurate after all. For all my fighting to change the fate she'd foretold, this was where it had brought me—right into its clutches.

As my arms jerked backward in a futile attempt to distance myself, my right hand knocked against a weight in my robe pocket. A weight that I hadn't realized I still carried with me. My shaking hand dug into the pocket and withdrew the small vial Arron had given me outside Breccan's cave. Although made of glass, it had miraculously survived all this time.

Staring down at the swirling, light blue liquid, Hortencia's last words shrilled in my mind:

*"When the road forks, your route will be clear. Either a destroyer or hero of realms you shall be."*

As the black mist thickened into a fog and began to glide toward me, it couldn't have been clearer that this was my fork in the road. Once it reached me, the Elder would surround me just as it had done when I was a newborn. Only this time, it wouldn't leave me.

As for my route… the oracle had said that there would be two.

But in my eyes, there was only one.

Forcing open the glass vial, I shut my eyes and thrust the opening to my lips. I filled my mouth with the elixir and took rapid gulp after gulp. It felt like acid on my tongue, burning down my throat as I swallowed.

A bloodcurdling scream emanated from the black fog and it gathered speed, but as I forced down the last of the liquid, the Elder was too late.

# Chapter 31: Vivienne

Derek and Sofia still hadn't returned. I knew how much it would mean to my brother to be here for the birth of my child. It saddened me to think that he'd likely miss it. Corrine was expecting my waters to break at any time. She'd been in and out of the room all day, and she was due to pay another visit within the next hour to check in on me.

As I rested in my and Xavier's bed, I looked down at my large stomach, protruding beneath a cotton nightgown. Xavier leaned against the headboard next to me on the mattress, his arms around me, gently stroking my belly. Liana sat in a rocking chair on my right. No words could express the joy I'd felt to be reunited with my best friend again. Of course she'd been thrilled to see that I was expecting a baby. I could still hardly believe that she was here, returned with Cameron and her two beautiful children. And yet, as we talked that night, my mind kept drifting elsewhere.

I couldn't shake the feeling that something on our island wasn't... right. But at the same time I could not quite put a finger on what it was. I felt a deep sense of unrest, and my dreams had been strange of late. My brother Lucas kept recurring in them. Lucas had died almost twenty years ago. I rarely dreamt or even thought much about him these days. My older brother seemed like a lifetime away—and for the most part, that former life was one I wished to forget.

Then, as we had stood near the Port bidding farewell to Derek, Sofia and the rest before they embarked on their journey with the dragons, I could have sworn that I saw a long, bodiless shadow on the beach nearby. Standing. Watching. But then I'd blinked, and it was gone.

When Derek had asked me what was the matter, I'd shrugged it off as simply me being sensitive due to my pregnancy. And really, perhaps that was all that it was.

"Viv!" Liana gasped, shooting to her feet. She was staring down at the bedsheets. "Your water has broken."

Xavier leapt up to examine them as I looked down. Liana was right.

"We need to go to Corrine!" Xavier exclaimed, his irises shimmering with excitement. He scooped me up in his arms and carried me out of the penthouse. Descending in the elevator and arriving on the forest ground, Xavier swept me along the tree-lined path.

Anticipation and nervousness filled me. As much as I'd learnt about childbirth since Xavier and I had conceived, there was just no way to fully prepare myself for the experience. I tightened my grip around my husband's neck and pressed my lips against his jawline. *At least I have my love by my side.*

As we passed the Port on our way to the witch's home, I caught a glimpse of the ocean and the hunters' naval ships in the distance. I wasn't sure whether it was just a product of my imagination, or of the frenzy my mind had gone into at the thought of meeting my child, but I could have sworn that I spied another long, dark shadow sweeping across the jetty. Then Xavier turned a corner, and my eyes were drawn away.

Whether or not I'd imagined it, I realized then that there was more to my urgency for Derek to return than just for him to meet his newborn niece or nephew.

I didn't feel safe with my brother and the dragons gone.

# WHAT'S NEXT?

Dear Shaddict,

With Christmas approaching, I have TWO exciting new releases for you to mark in your calendar!

## 1st ANNOUNCEMENT: CHRISTMAS SPECIAL!

I'm thrilled to announce the launch of a brand new story, and one many of you have been patiently waiting for ever since the dragon shifters arrived in The Shade … A Shade of Dragon!

Yes! You will finally get a story dedicated to the mysterious dragon prince, Theon, aka Master of "the artistry of romance", on his search for a maiden capable of bearing his love.

Where did Prince Theon go after leaving The Shade the night of Rose's wedding? What is really up with these heartstoppingly sexy fire-breathers? What was the "series of unfortunate events" that led them to become barren of their own females? Why are they so desperate for Theon to find a human mate? And will he ever find one?

These questions and more will be answered in A Shade of Dragon… Releasing December 8th 2015!

Visit www.bellaforrest.net for details on ordering your copy now!

You won't want to miss this ;)

Here's a preview of the smoking cover:

# 2nd Announcement:
# BEN & RIVER'S STORY CONTINUED!

The second release is the next part of Ben and River's story: A Shade of Vampire 21: A Vial of Life!

It releases just in time for Christmas: December 22nd 2015!

Pre-order your copy now from Amazon!
And here's a preview of the gorgeous cover:

This Christmas is going to be a thrill ride! I can't wait to meet you back in the world of The Shade…

Thank you for reading.

Love,

Bella x

P.S. Join my VIP email list and I'll send you a personal reminder as soon as I have a new book out. Visit here to sign up: **www.forrestbooks.com**
(You'll also be the first to receive news about movies/TV show as well as other exciting projects coming up!)

P.P.S. Follow The Shade on Instagram and check out some of the beautiful graphics: @ashadeofvampire
You can also come say hi to me on Facebook: www.facebook.com/AShadeOfVampire
And Twitter: @ashadeofvampire
I'd love to hear from you.

Made in the USA
San Bernardino, CA
21 December 2015